T0148891

Internet Interactive Reader -
Dead Men Dwarf at Winsor Ruins

Dwarf at Winsor Ruins

Product Utility
K - 12 Compliant
Critical Thinking
Knowledge Comprehension
Application Analysis Synthesis
And EVALUATION.
Available At Trafford publishing.com./ Also In E Book
Executive Editor\ Education Specialist: Dr. Jamie L Lial
STUDENTS STARR TEST STUDY DIRECTORY LINKS ENGLISH
AND SPANISH

Grades 4 to 11th

MADE IN USA

President Barack Obama

"As we began the 21st century, education
is first. For no child to be left behind
is .paramount, head start to college. Step up."

 www.trafford.com
North America & international
toll-free: 844-688-6899 (USA & Canada)
fax: 812 355 4082

Dead Men Dwarf at Winsor Ruins

Author Parker Chamberlain
Illustrator Parker Chamberlain

Episode I

Black Dwarf

MISSISSIPPI

Preface
of
Winsor Ruins
Calborne County, Mississippi

Windsor Ruins

The **Windsor Ruins** are located in Claiborne County in the U.S. state of Mississippi, about 10 miles southwest of Port Gibson near Alcorn State University. The ruins are those of the largest antebellum Greek Revival mansion built in the state, and have been used in various motion pictures.

History

The Windsor Plantation at one time covered 2,600 acres (11 km²). Smith Coffee Daniell II, who was born in Mississippi in 1826, the son of an Indian fighter turned farmer and landowner, constructed the mansion itself in 1859-1861. In 1849 he married his cousin Catherine Freeland (1830-1903) by whom he had three children.

Basic construction of the house, which was designed by David Shroder (Shroder also designed and built Rosswood, which is located in Lorman) was done by slave labor. The bricks for use in the 45 foot columns were made in a kiln across the road from the house. The columns were then covered with mortar and plaster. There were 29 of these columns supporting the projecting roof line with its plain, broad frieze and molded cornice. This provided protection for the galleries that encompassed the house at the second and third levels. The fluted columns had iron Corinthian capitals and were joined at the galleries by an ornamental iron balustrade.

Skilled carpenters were brought in from New England for the finished woodwork and the iron stairs, column capitals and balustrades were manufactured in St. Louis and shipped down the Mississippi River to the Port of Bruinsburg several miles west of Windsor.

The mansion cost about $175,000.00 (this would be about 3.5 million dollars today) to build and was completed in 1861. However Smith Daniell lived in the home only a few weeks before he died at the age of 34.

When completed, the home contained over 25 rooms, each with its own fireplace and, among other innovations, featured interior baths supplied with water from a tank in the attic.

On the Main floor, flanking the broad hall, were the master bedroom, a bath, 2 parlors, a study and the library. In the ell off this part of the structure was located the dining room.

Windsor Ruins
U.S. National Register of Historic Places
Mississippi Landmark

Location:	Claiborne County, Mississippi
Nearest city:	Port Gibson, Mississippi
Coordinates:	31.942327°N 91.12994°W
Built/Founded:	1859-61
Governing body:	Mississippi Department of Archives and History
Added to NRHP:	November 23, 1971
Designated	October 11, 1985[1]

A Word from the Author

Construction on Oakland Memorial Chapel began in 1840 by Dr. Jeremiah Chamberlain, Oakland College's founder and president. It was completed in 1851 two years after the death of Dr. Chamberlain. While this structure was consistently referred to as The Chapel, the building also housed recitation and library rooms, space for philosophical and chemical apparatus, and an observatory in the cupola. Oakland Chapel united the religious and academic activities of the college in one building.

Statement from Bethel Church:

"Chamberlain envisioned Oakland College educating the 300,000 inhabitants of Mississippi, Louisiana and Arkansas." Representatives of three Louisiana parishes and eight Mississippi counties met at Bethel Church in January 1830, and approved Chamberlain's proposal to establish an 'Institution of Higher Learning under the care of Mississippi Presbytery.' While its founders were searching for a permanent location, the school opened with three students on May 14, with Dr. Chamberlain serving as President. By July 1830, 250 acres had been given to Oakland College and construction of the first buildings began. The early years of Oakland College were characterized by growth and optimism. The optimistic future of Oakland was severely curtailed with the death of its founder and president, Dr. Jeremiah Chamberlain in 1851. **Chamberlain, an ardent Unionist and Whig, was assassinated on campus by a Secessionist.** Following Chamberlain's death, Oakland moved into a period of slow growth. Oakland College's final decline was precipitated by the Civil War.

As a writer, I selected a portal hole view of the many childhood adventures surrounding the rich historical and cultural aspects of this time period and location. I selected this short story because it combines a brief history of my family roots, a plantation that represents the beginning of black education in my home state and the center of southern tradition and individual states rights which changed the future of former slaves, their children and great grandchildren. **Julia Chamberlain, my older sister, is one of these**

DAVID L. GREEN

District 96: Adams,
Amite, Pike, Wilkinson

3519 Berwick
Cassels Rd.
Gloster 39638
(601) 225-4494

House 1980 – 2005. Born October 14, 1951, in Rosetta. Gloster High, Southwest Mississippi Junior College. Retail merchant. Baptist. Mason, Eastern Star, Shriner, Heroines of Jericho, Voters League, NAACP, former deputy sheriff and city police officer. Widower; one child. Democrat. Served on the following committees: Fees and Salaries of Public Officers (Chmn.); Appropriations; Investigate State Offices; Management; Select Committee on Fiscal Stability; Transportation; Wildlife, Fisheries and Parks.

STATE REPRESENTATIVE, DISTRICT 96

County	David L. Green (D)
Adams	.771
Amite	.2,830
Pike	.314
Wilkinson	.3,135
TOTAL	.7,050
PERCENTAGE	.100.0%

Alcorn State University at a Glance

1830 Oakland Memorial Chapel, famed landmark and oldest building on the campus, was constructed. Here, in 1831, the first degree issued by a Mississippi institution was confer

1830 Belle Lettres, Dormitory Two, and Dormitory Three, also historical landmarks, were constructed.

1830 President's Home erected.

1871 Oakland College property purchased by State of Mississippi.

1871 Hiram R. Revels elected President.

1871 Alcorn University created by an act of the Mississippi State Legislature on May 13.

down line slave descendants who attended Alcorn State University, who graduated at the top of her class. **Julia attained a master's degree in education; the first of Parker and Hester Chamberlain's five daughters to graduate Magna Cum Laud. She became a teacher in Gloster, Mississippi, a small town south of Lorman, Mississippi.** Her education gave birth to a marriage, with a young man named David Green. David served his country as a soldier in the United States Army. Julia's education enabled her to assist David in focusing his time and energy into a political career that spanned for four decades. David ran against the Great White Opposition in a state wide election for district ninety-six which consists of four counties, and won the state election that landed him his victory in the Mississippi legislature. A position never before obtained by a black man. This became possible when Martin Luther King challenged the Voting Rights Act of 1963 and 1964 and won approval into law by the U.S. Congress, and signed by President John F. Kennedy, these laws made it possible for downline slave descendants to become beneficiaries of the civil rights bill which allowed minorities like David Green equal rights to run for public office. **The Honorable David Green was elected by the people of Mississippi as a State Representative for these four counties, Amite, which is Liberty MISS, the town of Centerville and town of Gloster, Wilkenson, County Seat Natchez MISS.** These are large communities in the state of Mississippi.

This story is one of many successful careers that grew from slave descendants of poor cotton tenant farmers. Parker Chamberlain, my great grandfather was born under slavery in Mississippi. He was a field hand, carpenter and a wagon builder. He was a young man when President Abe Lincoln abolished slavery. Parker Chamberlain witnessed the turn of the century from the 1880's to the 1900's. My father, Parker Chamberlain II, son of a minister and farmer, knew the value of education. It was my mother and grandmother who applied the push to each one of my sisters Ann-r.i.p., Julia, Thrasher, Dorothy, and Venester Chamberlain to finish high school and attend college. My great, great grandmother Lucinda Chamberlain was a congregation member of a church called Bethel which was held outdoors under four Poplar trees and a preaching stone on the south forty acres of Windsor Plantation in 1860 before Alcorn College was chartered in 1871. My great grandmother, Mila Chamberlain was a student at Alcorn College after it was chartered. My grandmother Julie Coffey James was a teacher at Alcorn in the late 1930's and 1940's. Alcorn has now grown into **Alcorn State University located in Lorman, Mississippi** and is one of the largest minority universities in the state of Mississippi.

This is a story of transition from the 1930's continuing through the 1970's. The short story I have written describes only the enjoyable side of the historic development that took place during my childhood. As an author, I have focused on the simple joys of growing up in 1963-1967, such as, a treasure hunt and travels with my Uncle George and Aunt Corine Wolf and cousins on the back drop of the Winsor Plantation ,and the surrounding plantation towns, PORTRODNEY, PORTGIBSON,LORMAN,REDLICK,HARRISTOWN,FAYETTE,EMERALD MOUND,GRAVEL HILL,POUPLAR HILL,DOW PLANTATION, JOHN NOBL PLANTATION,SMITHS PLANTATION SCOTTS PLANTATION AND BIG RED AT COON-BOX-FORK PLANTATION.

The correlation of education and slave descendants is that the slaves were not allowed to be educated or congregate by many plantation owners during the antebellum periods. They were only allowed by some plantation owners to worship God. It was a crime to educate slaves in some states, punishable by death.

However, there were some exceptions that allowed slaves to meet. Winsor was one of those exceptions that allowed their slaves to meet in the woods on the south forty acres of Winsor Plantation, in a place called Four Poplars. Four Poplars was where they met for church. The minister would stand on a moss covered granite stone to preach the word of God to his fellow slaves.

Slavery required clean communication; communication that required linguistic conversion by slaves from Ebonics to English. This required teaching the alphabet to the slaves using a Holy Bible. Education through religion gave birth to a preaching stone, developed into a one room shack, for teaching God's word to slave children. The wife of the plantation owner, at Windsor realized the value of teaching English to the slave children and expanded her communication from the slave children to the adult slaves.
The adult slaves slowly learned Ebonics then merged to English. However, some slaves spoke Portuguese, Greek, Spanish, broken Ebau, Yemen and many other languages brought from the countries they were captured from.

Communicating through religious scripture was used to teach the slaves English and became a crucial part in the plantation daily operations.

Over time the education of the slave became an absolute necessity for plantations to operate successfully. Winsor became a super plantation. My Uncle Guy, son of a down line slave, was employed by Alcorn State University as a corn crop inspector.

We were children having fun in a place that our great, great grandparents were held as property and tied to the land, land that has our most precious blood spilled and tilled into the soil. **It is true that the people had their feet in the Mississippi mud and Mississippi blood.**

Bibliography of Julia Green

Julia Chamberlain Greene/gradute of Alcorn State University Magna Cum Laude, master degree in education minor in Biology, scientist, teacher at Gloster High Gloster, Mississippi, political activist co. Campaign Manager for the honorable David Green, Eastern Starr Prince Hall, Alpha Kappa Alpha Sara, Avid Democrat, Southern Baptist. 1947 to 1995, transcended.

UNIQUE FACTS OF THIS STORY

The story of The Honorable David Green and Julian Chamberlain Green is one of many TRUE AMERICAN EXPERIENCES. David Green's career as a State Representative spanned three decades in the Mississippi legislature is a true story. David attended Alcorn State University which was established by the Mississippi legislator on May 13, 1871. And David Green was elected by the people as a State Representative a hundred and nine years later.

The Honorable David Green is a down line slave's son. He made his historical journey into our nation's history books as the first black State Representative in 1980 to serve these counties and towns. Adams county, which county seat is Natchez, Amite county which is Glouster and Centerville Mississippi, Pike county which is McCome Mississippi, and Wilkinson County which is Woodville Mississippi. As a black representative, David is the first in the history of the state of Mississippi to represent these counties as a legislator. **The Honorable David Green also is the first State Representative that attended Alcorn State University and was elected to the legislator which is the original state body that chartered the University in 1871.** This is a historical event in itself. Mississippi historically is the heart of southern state's rights.

This is proof positive that education and political activeness has changed one of the most prejudiced of states into a modern, semi- socially equal Mecca. Education has also changed the face of America from forty acres and a mule to Barrack Obama, America's first black President. Completing the circle that began with Mrs. Sadie Hawkins women's suffrage movement, to Mrs. Harriett Tubman's Underground Railroad, to Mrs. Rosa Parks Freedom Riders, and then to Dr. Martin Luther King's, "I have a dream speech" that America is one of the greatest nations on earth because she can change.

The primary story of Dead Men Dwarf at Windsor Ruins is semi-fictional. It contains some true events of the authors early childhood.
The Legend of Blue Water Treasure is purely fictional, its primary purpose is a teaching tool; an example of subversion and a demonstration of Jim Crow politics on a simple farm community to demonstrate the oppressive tactical effect.

Dead Men Dwarf
at Winsor Ruins

By Parker Chamberlain

Cast and Critters

Grand Paw: George Wolf

Uncle Guy: Guy Wolf

Nunny Lee: Guy Wolf's wife

BreDear: Parker Chamberlain Jr., Myself

Loon: Ana Banks

Winky: Will Banks

Old Mann: James Banks Jr.

Pappy: James Banks Sr.

Nasa: Venester P. Chamberlain

Lord Winsor:

There are 201 characters in the Barnyard Crew they are not listed by name.

Lord Chamberlain:

Chapter I

Loons
Treasure Hunt

Tomahawk Farms

Uncle Guy was outside waiting for us at his house on the South side of Winsor Plantation, which is now Alcorn State University. His house was located in the middle of a cornfield. The university provided him with a home, as he worked for the university as a crop inspector for the Agra-Business department. We arrived in the back of a 1954 Chevy pickup truck. Cousin Loon was a stringy looking eleven year old with buck shots of hair that were a quick reminder of her temperament. Loon was the sister of James Banks Jr., lovingly called Old Mann, his brother, Will Banks was nicknamed Winky. These were my childhood playmates that formed a large part of my country escapades, drawn to a backdrop of river towns, beginning with Port Vicksburg, Port Gibson, Lorman, Port Rodney and Fayette, Mississippi. My hometown of Vicksburg taught me city living and other late twentieth century ways, merging with an eighteenth century mist of social oppression and social change

Loon, Old Mann, Winky, my sister V (who we called Nasa) and I (given name Parker, but called Bredear) were piled in the truck telling jokes and poking fun for thirty-five miles to Uncle Guy's house. As we banged and clattered down the potholes, Loon's buck shots were making a swishing sound as the wind passed through her hair, giving her the look of Medusa, the fable Greek goddess, to look at her would turn you to stone.

We spent many moments teasing Loon calling her Stone face. We arrived with chattering teeth and vibrating lips from the potted, potholed, gravel road, the truck came to a smooth stop, Gramp's door cracked open and we hopped out. The smell of fresh cooked bacon, eggs and the aroma of corn and sweet onion filled the moist morning air.

Tomahawk Farms

Two blue tick hounds named "You Know" and "I Know" greeted us with growling and howling as we approached the front steps, we were soon reminded that strangers must not go into the house until invited.

They took great joy at nipping at our heels and toes, if we attempted to enter Uncle Guy's house without escort. We all peered at the shotgun house with a large white picket fence, red, white and blue windmills lazily spinning in the wind and four large birdhouses swaying on long poles.

We received warm hugs as we approached the steps by Aunt Nunny Lee, a narrow wisp of a woman with big, round green Cajun eyes. Skinny as a rail, she welcomed each one of us children into her living room. It was a place of beautiful shelves of angels, Aunt Jamima ceramics, and nursery rhyme ceramics. Little Jack Horner, eating cherry pie, Pus in Boots, Little Boy Blue, Hey diddle, diddle the Cat and the Fiddle, the cow jumped over the moon, and may others filling each corner of the room. In the center of the room was a black Ben Franklin wood burning stove, well maintained and quiet for mid June.

There was a cool breeze blowing through the back door past the McCormick wood range carrying with it the smell of fresh fried bacon, and other goodies that had flooded our senses before our entry.

We were anxious to get outside to play and find the barn to see what adventures were waiting to be found or what treasures were hidden in the woods and forest beyond the boundaries of the tree line and corn fields.

"You guys want breakfast?" asked Uncle Guy.

With big smiles we spoke all at once, "yeah, we're starved!" We all headed for the kitchen table, set in a red and white checkerboard square tablecloth. Breakfast was Deep South grits, eggs, bacon, biscuits, coffee, buttered toast and fresh cut roasted corn.

"While you fellas are out playing, stay away from the Winsor Crossing, don't get on the old bridge and don't go near the plantation ruins. There have been some strange happenings going on down there, sink holes and animals disappearing.

The Big Red Barn

Lord Winsors Treasure

I lost four cows and three pigs to those ruins. So, stay away! You can play anywhere else but watch for snakes, 'cause this is Copper Head and Rattlesnake country," exclaimed Uncle Guy.

As we all laughed Old Mann said with his snaggle tooth grin, "we be snake killa's!" Loon danced on her stick legs a two step gig with her buck shots and tiny red barrettes jiggling looking like a pixie, she cried out, "we be snake killa's!"

Winky followed Loon's two step gig exclaiming, "we be treasure hunta's and snake killa's!" Round and round they danced until everyone laughed at the sight. They looked like two skinny little monkeys dancing.

Belly whopping laughter erupted and we ran out the back door towards Big Red, the barn, our favorite meeting place to plan our treasure hunts. From the top of the barn, we had the perfect view of any person approaching Big Red.

[1] Loon said, "Winsa is supposed to have Dead Man Gold hid by the Lod Winsa himself. My Pappy says he killed ten black slaves to protect his treasure until he come back to claim it. Pappy says Lod Winsa said, 'in the blood of all you does you swear to protect all my holdings in life and death to use the demon power in creation any means necessary until I Lod Winsa call you back and release you.' 'Ye-sa Lod Winsa,' the slaves replied. With ten shots, all ten were laid clockwise around the treasure and each sprinkled with white devil dust so the ten souls belong to him and all his kin."

Nasa asked, "Loon, is you crazy?! You expect us to go up against dust devils and the likes to find this treasure?"

Winky's eyes were as big as marbles and shaking from fear, his voice whispering, "two years ago, me and Pappy was looking for Unca Guy's cows and stumbled on to the old grave of dead Bon Jim, Lod Winsa, the master in charge of all slaves. We found his name carved in the Dwarf Tree on the south forty acres of the plantation. Pappy looked around and found nine broken swords stuck in the ground with only the handles sticking up in a circle."

Winky's eyes had grown to the size of balloons now and his voice sunk lower, "Pappy started to dig at the first sword, he got ten shovels of dirt moved, and then all of a sudden there was whistling and howling at high speed through the air as though being hurled by a million rock slingers. The Dwarf Tree itself climbs, twisted clockwise at the base which was eight feet thick, the limbs cracked and popped twisting upward and it began to lean all the way over the grave site. Pappy looked at me and said 'we's found it and no matter what you see or hear don't pay it no mind; the evil spirits are just trying to scare us away.' Pappy looked back in the hole he was digging and screamed, 'O Lod, there's a zillion spiders and snakes down here!' He hopped sideways out of the hole, I looked behind me and there was a big 2,000 pound Black Angus bull with blood red eyes and blood dripping from his mouth with fire surrounding him. Pappy's feet was spinning, so was mine and we ran so fast the soles of our shoes came off."

There was loud roaring laughter from Loon, Nasa, Bredear and Winky. Old Mann was belly laughing and rolling on the barn floor.

In defense Winky said, "Pappy was running so fast he jumped three barbwire fences. We looked back and the black bull disappeared and there was no stopping Pappy or me from running like crazy. When we got across the field and stopped to catch our breath Pappy said, '"look, we saw a swarm of little white balls of light the size of golf balls moving in a circle around the Devil Tree." Pappy and I hobbled toward home with swollen feet, scared as rabbits. Pappy said, "boy them spirits is bad, they are more powerful than anything I ever seen. We need us a fire and brimstone preacher! Yeah boy, we need Reverend Jo Henry Brown and his helper John P. Lee. They know how spirits think and have devil dust that they can't cross and they have some magic potions that will help get the dead man's gold!'"

Winky said, "You know Loon, Pappy died before he could go back so it's up to us to go and get the gold. We need Jo Henry and John P. Lee."

Chapter II

Holy Men
Witches Brew
&
Spit Fire

Loon rolled her eyes in a circle and said, "All us need is the Bible, Holy water, a sack of devil dust, some Cat Balou and Chigga powder, and eight skinny black elbows, a digging, sure enough."

Nasa asked Loon, "Is you crazy? The devil don't give a cat's tail about no Holy water. We need a fire and brimstone Holy man. Reverend Jo ain't gonna come today or tomorrow so's what in the heck ya'll fretting for. The only way to get rid of them haunts and evil spirits today is ghost powder and witch brew. The Holy Bible, a whole slew of crosses, a keg of prayer water and a gallon of corn whiskey to pour on the graves to keep them drunk until we gets the gold."

Loon said, "We's got to pray up a storm and chew a half cut of a day's work tobacco for spittin' them spirits away and dash the Holy water all around in a circle of that Devil Tree and stick fifteen of them crosses outside the Holy water circle and ten crosses round them graves with the swords to hold them spirits in the graves. Then pour salt around each grave so's they can't get out to scare the dickens out of us."

"Loon, where the heck you going to get tobacco?" asked Winky.

Loon reached in her skinny little v-neck blouse and retrieved a full cut of a day's work of tobacco and her round eyes rolled sideways with a snaggle tooth smile and said, "Grand Pappy won't miss it." With a skinny leg, gig hop she reached under her dress and produced the salt box from the breakfast table and with half a frog leap hip hop she crossed the barn floor and opened the tool shed. She grabbed two shovels, two large cotton sacks, two pick axes, a keg of corn whiskey, two gallons of Holy water and a bag of devil dust with a cross bone and skull with three X's.

Old Mann yelled, "Loon, where the heck did you get all this stuff? You know Grand Pappy is going to kill you if he finds out about his missing tobacco!"

Loon danced a double gig looking like a black long legged spider monkey. "We's gonna be rich! We's snake killa's, ghost killa's, and holy rollies." Everyone joined in the singing, "snake killa's, ghost killa's, ooh la la, snake killa's, ghost killa's, ooh la la." Loon was gig

hopping in a circle and it was a sight to see. Loon yelled, "Come on ya'll! Let's demon stomp and devil stomp to keep them spirits in the ground!"

Winky locked his arm in Loon's and they looked like two spider monkeys dancing in a circle. Old Mann joined in, then Nasa all chanting, "snake killa's, ghost killa's, ooh la la, holy rollies, holy rollies, ooh la la, holy rollas, holy rollas-ooh-la-la. Snake killa's, ghost killa's, ooh la la. Ghost dust, ghost dust, ooh la la, devil dust, devil dust, oh my gosh, dead men, dead men, ooh la la, holy rollas, holy rollas stay in the squash!"

BreDear jumped in, "Hey! How ya'll going to get God to okay this holiness?" You could hear a pin drop when I said that, the gig stopped. Every eye, as big as spittoons, looked dumbafied. There was mumbling and whispering among the group.

"Yeah Loon, what if God don't throw in with this hunt for treasure?" Nasa asked.

"Then we's going to pray up a storm until he throws in," responded Loon. "Now on ya knees sinnas." Loon reached under her dress and brought out a blue royal Masonic Bible, Prince Hall Edition. "Ya'll sinnas form a circle," Loon directed.

We all went to our knees, and chanted long and loud, "yes, Lod hear our prayers, we's a calling you Lod to help us this day. Lod, we's poor children and need you to help run these ghosts and devils straight to Hell. We's begging Lod to help the Holy Spirit to wrap around us right here and right now. We's your humble servants Lod and we wants to be rich, humble, servants Lod. We's going to give to build a church for them poor people who don't know you Lod. We's going to give a whole lot back for your glory Lod."

BreDear prayed, "Lord, Please hear our prayer. Knock and the door shall be opened, seek and ye shall find, ask and it shall be given to you now, Lod." All of a sudden we heard the sound of distant thunder. Loon opened one eye, eyeball rolling around in a circle saying, "He answered, Lod, Lod, he answered." Distant

Chapter III

Big Black Oreo's

thunder clapped three more times, then two and then slow distant rolling thunder.

Loon flew into a hop leaping frenzy and looked like a spider monkey hopping from tree to tree. Winky locked arms and got into to the frenzy head bobbing, going around and around on pixie stick legs. Old Mann with skinny legs flying, shoe leather flopping, coverall hanging by one strap, locked arms and joined the frenzy. "Good Lod have mercy, good Lod have mercy! We called you on that royal telephone, good Lod so have mercy," we chanted. We danced and then Nasa jumped in the fling and joined us.

BreDear asks Loon, "What makes you think he answered you?"

The dancing stopped and you could hear a pin drop.

Loon replies, "there ain't a cloud in the sky so what else could it be?" She chants, "Thank you Lod, oh thank you Lod. Lod hears us, yes sir he sure did hear us so let's go." We set off on the adventure, Loon with Bible in hand, and Winky with shovel in one hand, cotton sack over his right shoulder. Nasa grabbed the Holy water and the keg of corn whiskey. BreDear took the salt and the sack of thirty crosses. We headed out the back of the barn and across the sun lit meadow along the pig trail into the woods across from the bubbling brook, up the rolling hills and in the valley into the black forest. One hour later we emerged at the Winsor Crossing Rail road. The big black bridge was a stone's throw away and Loon was eyeing the bridge nervously. "Well we's here but let's have a snack before we cross," she suggested.

She removed the sack and Winky opened it. It contained a box of saltines, a roll of red summer sausage, a package of cinnamon rolls, four tins of red kippers, four pints of jungle juice and a half pack of Oreo cookies. Loon laid out a little blanket of napkins and on each napkin she put six crackers, and broke a quarter piece of summer sausage for each and one cinnamon roll. Also, she placed three kippers and one pint of juice. She prayed, "Lod bless these vittles and these drinks on Jesus name as quick as we can eat them, amen." We ate lunch quickly and quietly, looking forlornly at the bridge. We were apprehensive, yet determined. We wrapped

Chapter IV
The Corner Stone

up lunch and repacked the sacks and began to cross the bridge at Winsor Crossing. As we crossed the bridge, its broken board brought fear of slipping through to mind. The combined weight of our walking made the bridge ripple like a snake in motion. We quickly crossed the old bridge; we could see the white tips of Winsor in the distant skyline. Swarmed by black crows squawking lazily about it as though they were saying "go back, go back." The midday sun was warm against our faces as we headed across the black bridge. The tracks were narrow and worn from the steam engines that passed them over for the last hundred years. Loon was leading the pack with her stick legs and buck shots waving happily in the wind as we marched to our tune of, "snake killa's, ghost killa's, snake killa's, ghost killa's, snake killa's, ghost killa's, here we come."

Over the meadow and across three barbwire fences, on the horizon I could see the sixteen white granite Roman Columns of Winsor Ruins gutted mansion and the black giant dwarfs that potted the plantation. These trees were beautiful green giants with low slung limbs that from a distance looked like hundreds of human arms, low to the ground protecting the massive eight hundred to one thousand year old trunks. Invisible from a distance, as we grew closer the trees became frightful, menacing giants giving off the smell of rotting flesh, caused by the leafy fauna that surrounds the base of the trees, as it decays producing a horrible stench. The plantation owner also hung runaway slaves caught stealing on the limbs of these giant trees until the body rotted away and fell to the ground. Thus, enforcing the trees named, "Dead men Dwarf." We looked across the field and noticed a heard of dairy cows pasturing away in between the fences.

We were approaching the Great Masonic Grave Yard of Winsor Monastery that had fallen in ruins from neglect and old age. Loon strode up to its cornerstone marker dated 1770 to Reverend Chamberlain and the congregation, inscribed; "The blessed bring chaos to order through divine prayer," engraved in stone the great Masonic Compass and Eastern Star Pinnacle, the Double Headed Eagle of the Sublime Prince, and the bottom symbol Order Knights Templars. Loon asked, "Okay Winky, where in thunder is that tree you and Pappy was digging from, huh?"

Winky looked around and eased his head around the side of the church looking south. He backed up to the church corner and leaned back on the stone as he raised his right arm to the horizon and counted as he stepped forward, "one, two, three, four, five, six, seven, eight, nine, ten, eleven, twelve, thirteen, fourteen," he looked down. He was standing at Lord Winsor's wife's crypt grave. It was black granite marked with a gold tip pyramid and the structure was engraved with an Eastern Star pinnacle and White Shrine and the Crown of Amananth, and a large winged gargoyle facing east, with its wings and fangs displaying a horrible menacing look. Winky rotated east following the gargoyle's glance, counting one hundred steps, we followed like mesmerized soldiers. We passed from the grave yard step by step and stone by stone. We weaved and walked across the black brook into the slaves' quarters. We passed the slaves graveyard into the Black Valley where we were suddenly aware of the disappearing sun light. On his one hundred and fiftieth step, we were standing in front of the largest, black dwarf tree we had ever seen. Peaking through the limbs, we could see its trunk was nine feet across and smelling of rotten flesh and dripping with thick, yellow-red goop.

"Yuck, whoa Nelly, she sure stinks," Winky said in a low voice. Eyes as big as the moon, he whispers in a shaky voice, "This is the tree."

Loon also replies in a low voice, "Whew, smells like ten zillion rotten fish and rotten eggs." She was shaking and Nasa had a crazy look on her face. Gripped at the sight and stench of the oldest living tree in the ruins, a fearsome sight of low hanging limbs, each as thick as three feet and curved like multiple serpents with millions of thick sappy dripping leaves that had saturated the surround soil with a mushy coating that smelled of rotten blood and other horrific stenches.

This African Dwarf tree seemed to be aware of our presence. Fear had griped each and every one of us. Loon, Old Mann, Winky, Nasa, and I were frozen in our tracks. It was as though the tree was silently telling us to run away.

Loon cried, "My God, my God, what an evil looking sight! The devil himself must have made this tree." With that said, she opened

her sack and slipped on her overshoes and waddled into the yellow-red goo that oozed from the dwarf tree. As we followed, Winky said, "Hand me the salt and devil dust, Old Mann. Two of them crosses but work fast because we be losing the sun light." In a flash Loon had circled and dusted five of the ten swords. Trembling fearfully, Winky was dusting and salting three of the swords. Old Mann was removing the tools from the sacks as fast as he could. The evening was charged with excitement. Nasa snapped to the task circling each sword with salt and the outer circle with devil dust. You could taste the fear and energy that charged the air. Bredear was sticking the white crosses in each prepared circle, we completed this task in fifteen minutes, shaking and eyeballing the dwarf tree every second, the air was so thick it was stifling.

Loon reached in her sack and removed a powder blue Masonic Bible and said, "We's ready, Old Mann get your pick and shovel, and you Nasa get that keg of corn whiskey and the gallon of Holy water, give it to BreDear. Pour that Holy water all the way around the outer edge of this tree and Nasa pour the whiskey outside BreDears circle and don't leave no gaps. If you leave a gap we be overrun with the ghosts, goblins and spirits." We hopped to the task and as I poured the Holy water, the ground began to smoke and boil and these tiny white lights began to pop out of the soil. On trembling legs, Nasa was just two steps ahead and six feet over, when thunder erupted from underfoot. She looked at me with panic, eyes large as softballs, trembling like a leaf, in a cyclone!

Loon yelled, "faster, this tree is waking up and she is gonna try to get ugly. As I began to pour the Holy water, the roots began to recoil as I poured it; they looked like snakes recoiling from fire. As the ground began to separate, the roots were recoiling with a whipping sound. The circle of Holy water was almost complete when a root ripped itself from the ground and popped like a whip, knocking the keg of corn whiskey from Nasa's hand. Nasa asked, "Oh Lod, what in the heck is this?" Loon yelled, "BreDear close that circle!" I dashed the Holy water on the root and it rolled up like a dead snake, closing the circle.

Chapter V

Dwarf Attack

Nasa crawling and shaking cried, "help me Lod, help me Lod, oh help me Lod!" She grabbed the keg off the ground and commenced to pour more whiskey then suddenly the dwarf tree itself began to twist and lay over, moving all of its limbs to block Nasa from completing the whiskey circle.

Limbs snapping, branches growing, the limbs began stretching, and cracking then the sound of ten million rocks flying through the trees whistling as though being thrown at the speed of sound. The loud roaring sounds had all of us shaking in our shoes. Nasa dashed the keg of corn whiskey to close the circle and ran towards BreDear. We listened as Loon read aloud the book of Exodus and dashed Holy water on the trunk of the dwarf tree as it recoiled from the onslaught.

Meanwhile, sweat flowing like a river, Old Mann and Winky were digging like mad men at the slave master's grave.

BreDear and Nasa stood inside the circles frightened and trembling eyes popping, as all heck broke loose around them, they stood their ground.

Loon was a sight to see standing within striking distance of the twisting and recoiling limbs, a forty foot limb snapped passed her head, retreating from the onslaught of her slinging Holy water.

Outside the circles, thousands of critters from the red eyed bull, cows, snakes, giant spiders, wolves, bears, lions, fanged baboons screaming, bursts of white light, tiny balls of white light, followed by screaming banshees, all running around the outer circle of Holy water, not a critter crossed the line. All the swords were vibrating and smoking in the ground. Huge white balls of light burst through the soil but the crosses held them in check. Loon yelled, "Winky, whatever you see, don't pay it no mind!"

Then, at that moment a hurricane of high velocity stones, bricks, and rocks whistled, very loudly passing us all around, not hitting anyone. Winky screamed, "It's getting busy over here." We looked and there appeared to be a brilliant ball of white light in the hole, at least five feet deep. Winky yelled, "oh Lod, oh Lod, we's got it, we's got it!" The next minute, the dwarf tree's limbs leaned over the hole and snapped the pick Winky was digging with in half. Old Mann was digging when a dark spirit came out of the treasure box and broke the steel tip of his shovel. Then, a huge cloud of black goo rose up and slung itself, blinding them both at once. At that moment Loon screamed, "Run for your lives, run for your lives!" She dropped the Bible, as goo flew like hot syrup. Nasa and I were slipping, and sliding like crazy. We looked back and all of the critters were chasing us. We looked like deer and gazelle hopping over the barbwire fences. I could hear the wind whistling past my ears and as we ran full gallop. Loon's little dress was floating over her knees and her barrettes had popped off her buck shots, Old Mann lost the soles of his boots. I saw one peel off as he cleared the second barbwire fence. We looked like a heard of impalas gliding over fences. Winky lost his cap and ran out of his coveralls. We hit Winsor Crossing at full gallop and you could hear our feet plop, plop, plop, like wild horses. We ran all the way to Big Red, the barn and did not look back.

Loon had run out of her stockings, Nasa lost a pair of brand new socks and shoes and rain galoshes. Winky lost his hat, coveralls, and his shirt. Old Mann's coveralls were ripped and his polka dot shorts were visible, he also lost his eyeglasses. BreDear lost his shoes, socks, hat and shirt. Sweating and breathless we all piled into the barn and collapsed on the floor into the hay, gasping for breath. We were all shaking like leaves for about thirty minutes.

Uncle Guy walked into the barn looked at us and said, "Ya'll be snake killa's, ghost killa's, and holy rollies... naw ya'll be chickens and ya'll be scared." He smiled, "well now I guess you'll listen to your elders when we say stay away. This is a lesson in humble obedience. I know you guys were not going to hear me. What have you learned? There's no place like home." We all laughed and walked to the house to eat supper. On the way to the house Uncle Guy said, "Have you heard of the treasure of Blue Water Falls?"

"Is that were Lod Winsa's brother buried his gold?" asked Loon.

"Na, Na Loon, we's had all the treasure huntin' we can stand," we all exclaimed.

"It ain't over, until it's over," Loon said, her buck shots bobbing, her head shaking, and looking buck eyed.

Uncle Guy asked, "What happened to your clothes?" Everyone laughed and said simultaneously, "we be snake killa's, ghost killa's, and ghosts got the best of us."

We all laughed and giggled leaving Big Red Barn chanting Snake killas Ghost killas, ooh la la, Snake Killas Ghost Klllas ooh la la Snake killas Ghost Killas bite yo paw. Winky was whirling in a circle as we walked Old Mann flipping head over heels, Loon hop scotting forward, nasa skipping in a circle progressively, I was gig hopping while uncle Guy cheered us on. You could smell supper in the air. BreDear thought to himself, "Ahhh, yellow corn bread, and the evening air was heavy with the smell of something roasting like beef or chicken."

The sun was slowly setting on the horizon in brilliant red, dark blue scattered clouds. You could see the scallywag's scattered across the brilliant sunset, flapping ever so slowly toward their nesting place high in the tree tops. The evening was upon us, and the critters of the night began their nightly hunts.

Loon said, "Lookie, lookie ya'll, them bats are strung out all the way to the moon, they be Loon Moon Bats."

"Lookie, its old Black Fang Gang bout, two million of them," said Old Mann.

"Theys on the prowl," said Winky.

"And that old moon sure is pretty ain't she," said Nasa.

Uncle Guy said, "Well ya'll best stay close to the house, the bats is vicious critters I found two of Big Lula's calves and two of Little Chica's piglets sucked to death by them blood thirsty critters. Old Black Fang is on my hunting list for Old Bessie, my shot gun. We's got some double mint buck shots for his hungry blackness, and that other Big Hootie Tootie Owl gang been killing my chickens. Wholesale day and night, they's gone buck wild on my little gray guineas. So ya'll stay close to the house and keep a close sharp eye out for my critters and if any of you see them, shoot first ask questions later. There is a shot gun at the kitchen door, the front door and one in each room, so don't miss."

"That's right, we gonna fry 'em and die 'em. Hook 'em and cook 'em. Spattered, scattered, and smattered if any we see 'em," said Old Mann.

"Uncle Guy you can count on us," giggled Winky and Loon.

We had reached the house, you could smell supper cooking and the aroma, caught us by the nose and dragged us straight to the kitchen.

Chapter VI

The Red Beastie
&
Black Fang

Black Fang

"Oowee," said Old Mann.

"Yeper Dapper," said Winky.

"Ohh yeah, ya'll smell that... mmmmm" said BreDear.

"We's hungry," said Old Mann.

Winky added, "We so hungry we could eat a owl, raw!"

Loon gig hopped, "we SO HUNGRY we could eat Old Black Fang and his gang of nastys."

We all found a spot at the table, as Aunt Nunny Lee severed dinner: sweet potatoes, brown rice, yellow corn bread, greens, field peas and a silver covered roasting pot sitting in the middle of the checker board square table cloth. Grand Paw said the grace, we all bowed our heads, "Lord hear our prayer, this food represents the body of the Savior, this drink his Holy Spirit, bless it fast as we can eat it. Amen,"

At that moment Loon lifted the lid on the silver roasting pot and a cloud of steam rose high above the table revealing a long nose possum, with a potato stuffed in his long sharp teeth. Loon was shocked; she flung the lid into the air, fell backwards and fainted, hitting the floor like a ton of bricks. Nasa squealed, and ran away from the table. Winky jumped back from his seat and said in a shaky voice, "What in God's name is that critter grinning with potato in his mouth, Aunt Nunny?"

All the adults burst into laughter, Loon had passed out, Winky had a rash look on his face, and Old Mann was trembling at the sight, with a fork in his hands ready to defend himself against the roasted critter on the table. Nasa ran outside, and BreDear was giggling and laughing at all the funny reactions. Uncle Guy said in a stifled laugh, "Ya'll act like you ain't never had stuffed possum."

Uncle Guy, Grandpa and Aunt Nunny began to feast on the red beast.

"Gimme a leg and his snout" Uncle Guy said.

Loon woke up and gagged herself out of the kitchen; Nasa was nauseated and would not return to the kitchen. They found the fruit bowl in the living room and ran outside with it. The adults were laughing at all of us being squeamish. The evening passed quietly after supper and we all went to bed laughing. After the event of supper, we all teased loon about falling out at the sight of stuffed possum, grinning with potato in his mouth. The evening slipped in to restful sleep as each of us was visited by Wikkun, Blinkuun and Nodd.

This story is continued in Blue Water Treasure at Winsor Ruins.

OUR STORY CONTINUES

ORDER YOUR COPY

---E-mail us at deadmendwarf@aol.com

To order Internet

query www.Traffordbooks.com 1-888-232-4444 or1-866-941-0370

Author Parker Chamberlain

Illustrator Parker Chamberlain

Published by

Publisher Number

EXPLORE OUR WEB SITE COMING SOON WWW DEAD MEN DWARF .COM

Episode 1 order WWW.TRAFFORD.COM

Episode2

Episode 3

Explore OTHER BOOKS AND E-BOOK BY PARKER CHAMBERLAIN

Bibliography: FOR DEAD MEN DWARF AT WINDSOR RUINS

AS THE AUTHOR I WISH TO EXPRESS MY THANKS TO THE CONTRIBUTORS LISTES BELOW

FOR THERE PHOTOGRAPHS PERIDIOCALS AND OTHER CONTRIBUTIONS THAT PROVIDED   REFERENCE INFORMATION FOR THE COMPLETION OF THESE BOOKS FIRST EDITON, SECOND EDITION AND THIRD EDITIONS, THANK YOU FROM

PARKER CHAMBERLAIN FOR HELPING ME PROVIDE ELEMENTS TO COMPLETE THESE WORKS OF ART.

1. NATIONAL PARKS SERVICE, PHOTOGRAPHS OF NATCHEZ TRACE PARKWAY AND PHOTO GALLERY OF HISTORICAL FARMS ALONG THE PARKWAY

2. US DEPARTMENT OF INTERIORS FOR PHOTO GALLERY, FARM HOMES AND BARNS OF AMERICA

3. MISSISSIPPI BATTLE FIELD TOUR PHOTO GALLERY OF WINDSOR RUINS AND ASSOCIATED PHOTOGRAPHS OF EMERALD MOUND ON THE NATCHEZ TRACE PARKWAY

4. US DEPARTMENT OF INTERIORS FOR PHOTO GALLERY PHOTOGRAPHS OF MOUNT LOCUST AND PHOTOS OF CHURCH STREET IN PORT GIBSON MISSISSIPPI

5. CATALINA GARCIA FOR PHOTOGRAPHS OF DWARF TREES AT WINDSOR RUINS

6. CATALINA GARCIA FOR PHOTOGRAPHS OF WINDSOR RUINS SIXTEEN COLUMNS

7. MISSISSIPPI BATTLE TOURS PHOTO GALLERY FOR CHURCH STREET PORT GIBSON MISSISSIPPI AND ALL BATTLE FIELD TOUR MARKER SIGNS UTILIZED FOR HISTORICAL VALUE

8. TRAVEL IMAGES.COM FOR PHOTOS OF PHAR MOUNDS FALL HOLLOW FOR FARM PHOTOGRAPHS

9. SHUTTER STOCK.COM FOR FARM PHOTOGRAPHS

10. THE HONORABLE DAVID L GREEN, STATE REPRESANTIVE MISSISSIPPI LEGISLATURE FOR FAMILY CONTRIBUTIONS FOR THE COMPLETION OF THIS WORK

11. MISSISSIPPI LEGISLATURE VIA INTERNET INFORMATION THAT PROVIDED HISTORICAL BACKGROUND FOR THIS WORK

12. ALL CORN STATE UNIVERSITY FOR PHOTOGRAPHIC HISTORY OF ITS DEVELOPMENT

13. CITY OF FAYETTE HISTORICAL CONTRIBUTION AND BIRTH PLACE OF THE AUTHOR PARKER CHAMBERLAIN FOR PHOTOGRAPHIC CONTRIBUTIONS

14. CITY OF VICKSBURG FOR PHOTOGRAPHIC CONTRIBUTIONS AS THE HOME OF AUTHOR PARKER CHAMBERLAIN

15. THE STATE OF MISSISSIPPI FOR PHOTOGRAPHIC OPPORTUNITY OF VICKSBURG BATTLE FIELD PHOTOGRPAHS ACQUIRED BY AUTHOR PARKER CHAMBERLAIN

16. TOWN OF LORMAN MISSISSIPPI FOR PHOTOGRAPHIC CONTRIBUTIONS OF LANDSCAPE PHOTOGRAPHS OF ALL CORN STATE UNIVERSITY

17. TOWN OF PORT RODNEY MISSISSIPPI FOR HISTORICAL BACKGROUND OF WINDSOR PLANTATION

18. US DEPARTMENT OF INTERIORS PHOTOS AND BACKGROUND OF PORT RODNEY AND WINDSOR RUINS

19. TOWN OF PORT GIBSON FOR PHOTOS OF CHURCH STREET AND THE FAMOUS PRESBETERIAN CHURCH WITH THE GOLDEN HAND AND ALL THE OTHER HISTORICAL CITY MARKERS THAT CONTRIBUTED TO THIS WORK OF ART

20. PHOTO GALLERY OF PARKER CHAMBERLAIN THAT CONTRIBUTED TO THE COMPLETION OF THIS WORK.

FROM PARKER CHAMBERLAIN

 THE AUTHOR OF DEAD MENS DWARF AT WINDSOR RUINS,

THANK YOU FOR YOUR CONTRIBUTIONS TO THE COMPLETION OF THIS WORK.

Special Thank You to
Rosa Parks
Civil Rights Activist

Self Development

Institute for

Rosa
Civil Rights
1950

Parks
Activist
2005

Illustrated: 6/1/10
by Parker Chamberlain

Getting Into The Flow:

Author: Parker Chamberlain

We Hope You Enjoyed Dead Men's Dwarf at Winsor Ruins!

"On The Road Home..."

Coffey/Coffie Family Reunion
July 2010 -Fayette /Natchez, Mississippi

The story of West James and Julia coffee James was lived out in this intrepid plantation house as you look at this picture it is a reminder that our lives and life works are finite ,as you look at this picture you don't see the years of barbe Q's, parties. Planting green gardens, picking tomatoes beans corn, okra, hide -n-go seek games we played happy and sad times. Those moments are compressed into our minds, the grand children of this couple. My grand children will only see this broken down rusting weathered hulk of a house in this book because time has erased this home but the families that were born in this home are flourishing scattered around America, Milton L. James and Shelly James .and Hester James Chamberlain are the down line slave descendants of the this family, that has produced Teachers, Doctors Lawyers, Dentist, politicians, and many others, because of REAL TREASURE, EDUCATION, OUR PARENTS, STEPPED UP, AND REMINDED THEIR CHILDREN, NEVER FORGET JIM CROW IS IMMORTAL, AND PREYS ON IGNORANCE.

About the Author

Parker Chamberlain was born during the late 50's in Fayette, Mississippi, during a time when Jim Crow was the most dangerous criminal in America, parker chamberlain is a, native of Vicksburg, Mississippi. He like most American witnessed the Vietnam war, the political destruction and assassination of John F Kennedy and Bobby Kennedy and the assassination of Dr. Martin Luther King, and hundreds of individual micro cosms of change, all across America, birth pains of change, political war, water gate. Iran kuntra scandal, the moon landing. Ten presidents elected and the most surprising event in American history, the 44th president elected to office Barack Obama, the first black American president, proof positive that education and political activeness and a life death struggle with Jim Crow politics, changed the civil rights and political face of a nation. At her best, stars and stripes waiving in the winds and her worst, fire hoses blasting people in the streets in Selma, Alabama in the 60s, witnessing these events, will make Parker Chamberlain a great author through the 21st century.

The Legend of Blue Water Treasure at Dead Men Dwarf

Episodes II, III and IV

Parker Chamberlain

The Legend of Blue Water Treasure
at
Winsor Ruins

Author Parker Chamberlain
Illustrator Parker Chamberlain
Editor: JAMIE L. LAIL

Published by:
Publisher number:

Episode II

President Barack Obama

"As we began the 21st century, education is
first. For no child to be left behind is
paramount, head start to college. Step up."

About the Author. Parker Chamberlain was born during the late 50's in Fayette Mississippi, during a time when Jim Crow was the most dangerous criminal in America, Parker Chamberlain grew up in Vicksburg Mississippi. He witnessed; Vietnam War, the Political Destruction, and assignation of John F. Kennedy and Bobby Kennedy and the assignation of Dr Martin Luther King; and hundreds of individual, Micro Cosums Of Change, all across America, Birth pains of change, political war, water gate the moon landing, Ten Presidents elected and the end result, the 44th president elected to office, Barack-O-bama, the first Black American President, proof positive that education and political activeness and life and a death struggle with Jim Crow, changed the political face of the nation. Parker Chamberlain witnessed the birth of new America in the 21st century; this exposure to America at her best and at her worst will make him a great story teller throughout the twenty first century.

About the book/Overview: Parker Chamberlain; brings to his readers every Childs Secret wish, a treasure hunt set to a historical back ground of southern plantation; legends, and the oldest and largest Plantation in Mississippi Winsor Ruins; this story has the flavor of Mark Twain's Huckel Berry Finn; a drop of Edgar Allen Poe's Darkness in Fiction. Parker Chamberlain in his Author's word utilized Julia and David green as living examples that down line slave descendants have obtained A unique place in American Politics and the communities in the state of Mississippi. The honorable David Green was elected to the Office of State Representative for District 96 and is a Graduate of Alcorn State University, this university was established by the Mississippi Legislature in 1871 he is a first graduate from this university as a down line slave descendant to be elected to public office to serve the community as from the very legislative body that chartered the first and largest black university in the history of the state of Mississippi since the civil war, this has never been possible before the 1963 and 1964 voting rights act was approved by John F. Kennedy and the Congress of the United States; these leaps and bounds, in social and political change that began with the emancipation proclamation from the 1800'S thru the 1900'S, brought political change and self realization to the Negros, that education was not just a dream, but a doorway that accessed the stair well to power in America; a clear message Unlocked by President Kennedy in the 1963 and 1964 Voting Rights Act, to young Black Americans that a turning point has been achieved. It began with **40 acres and a mule** and has climaxed at the 44th president, a Black American; **Barack-O-bama**, prooof positive that America has reached her turning point. Envoked by Dr. Martin Luther King I Have a dream, America has more work ahead. ¡Parke-Chamberlain has spun a beautiful story of the Achievement of the American Experience not a Fiction, but a true story of his families American experience. Touched by the divine the Real Hunt For Treasure is Education, Political Activeness in The Communities of Our America.

Key Words: For on Line Research Readers may use when Searching for your book In our on line book store.	Bed Time Stories, Legends, Treasure Hunts, Tall Tales, American Folk Lore, Tree Stories, Treasure, Water Legends, American tales, Ethnic Legends, Presidents/44th, Dead Men Dwarf.

Key Note/Treasure/Tag Line: The Legend Of Dead Men Dwarf At Winsor Ruin

TAG LINES:

The Legend of DEAD MEN DWARF ATWINSOR RUINS	Big BADD DWARF/BBD

TAG LINES.

SNAKE KILLAS
GHOST KILLAS
OOH-L A-LA

Free Preview: We were approaching the Great Masonic **Grave Yard** Of Winsor
Monastery that had fallen into ruins from neglect and old age Loon

THE LEGEND OF BLUE WATER TREASURE
AT Winsor Ruins

EPISODE II

Chapter VII
Jim Crows
Legacy

THE LEGEND OF BLUE WATER TREASURE
AT Winsor Ruins

616

617

618

619

620

621

622

623

624

625

626

627

628

629

630

THE LEGEND OF BLUE WATER TREASURE
AT Winsor Ruins

631
632

633   **'Twas a beautiful day as the sun climbed steadily in the sky over the lush**

634 **green fields of Winsor Ruins.** The deep blue sky filled the humming of bees,

635 chirping of birds and the sound of a steady cawing that could be heard in the

636 distance which quickly grew louder and louder as the distance of the birds grew

637 closer. These weren't your normal run of the mill birds. They were Royal black

638 crows. You could hear them as they grew closer poking fun at each other.

639   **Hilo said, "Hey Howie what are we doing for breakfast?"** Howie said,

640 "Yabba Dabba Doo, McDonalds." Hilo said, "The farm or the restaurant?" Howie

641 said, "The dumpsters are full this time of the morning." Fred said, "Where's

642 Dino?" Mirie said, "Biting Wilma." Laughter erupted among the crows. Howie said,

643 "These kids are never going to find the gold unless we tell them the secret." Fred

644 said, "Yeah well, you know what happened when you tried talking last time, you

645 almost got eaten by an owl. Those owls don't give a snout if you are guilty or not.

646 You best not tell Looney Loon anything about the curse of the Blue Water

647 Treasure."

648 **Nana said, "Your Grand Pappy told you not to tell 'Lil Chicharon the secrets.** You

649 know what happens when you talk." Hilo replied, "Yeah, my family will be eaten

650 by owls and wiped out by the black demons and I will be hunted till death or

651 eaten alive by Old Black Raven." Meme said, "Hey Howie, you're a good friend

652 with little Chicharon, maybe you could show her that the kids are digging in the

653 wrong places."

654 **Yucka, flying upside down said, "If you guy's tell 'Lil Chicharon anything**

655 **we are in trouble, all of us.** Those owls are relentless and crazy. We'll be hunted

656 day and night, till we are dead." Old Maggie said, "Look here, I will tell Poncho Fox

657 the truth, he's in love with 'Lil Chicharon if you know what I mean, and those owls

658 are afraid of Pancho, so they are not going to mess with him." Howie said, "You

659 know Maggie, you are right. Poncho Fox don't give a monkey's yak about no owls.

660 He will eat them. Let's find Poncho. Remember Maggie, do not get too close,

661 Poncho is always hungry, so stay out of reach or else we will be "seeing" you as

662 Maggie dung spot on the fox trail, laughter erupted and spread through the

663 Murder of crows.

664 **Old Maggie said, "Ya'll a bunch of scary cats. Poncho will not get**

665 **anything here except the truth about the treasure and the slick trick Lord**

666 **Winsor pulled.** He killed a hundred black slaves to fake the gold burial." Howie

667 said, "You know all that slickness of Lord Winsor. He killed another ten black

668 slaves at the second tree. Now no one knows were the gold is because he died in

669 the Civil War." Howie said, "Except us and the only reason we know is because of

670 Great, Great, Great Granddaddy Jim Crow." Mr. Gable said, "The true burial site

671 with two slaves is one mile away. That Lord Winsor was a real snake. He was

672 slicker than slick Willie." MoDeep said, "Yea, but he didn't know about the crow

673 factor, Great, Great, Great, Grand Pappy. MO DEEP ASK, what does a slick Willie

674 do? Yucca giggled loud "caw, cawwwww, cawwwwwwwwww, A Monica".

675 **Laughter erupted from all the crows. MoDeep continued, "They had an**

676 **eye on Lord Winsor's slickness.** They saw everything. Ha, I am hungry let's flop

677 over to Mickie D's and grab some grub. Those dumpsters are running over this

678 time of day."

679 **Lump said, "We are raiders of the lone dumpster, giddy up fellas.** Last one

680 to the dump eats crow, caw, caw." Splat said, "You all know, we should, tell 'Lil

681 Chicharon that Loon is digging in the wrong place for Winsor Gold." Lump said'

682 "Yea Splat and soon as you open your bib you and all your family is owl food.

683 Besides, humans are not worth the risk." MoDeep said, "Yeah Lump, Winkey did

684 save your tail and you from that chili can you got stuck on your head last year, just

685 before Poncho Fox showed up, did you forget?"

686 **Lump said, "No, I didn't forget.** It is risky but those owls aren't the worse

687 thing. You know the worse thing is that Black Raven. He's a real killer. His job is to

688 enforce the Winsor curse fellas and Old One Claw, his sidekick, is worse than the

689 blackest evil we ever seen. MoDeep said, "Yep." Mr. Gable said, "Yep." Splat said,

690 "Yep, we need more time to consider the risk, for you to tell 'Lil Chicharon to give

691 Loon the secret. That's too risky."

692 **Splat said, "Hey look, the dumpsters are empty at McDonalds."** Mr. Gable

693 said, "Hey, Taco's Bell's full. Hit it fellas." MoDeep said, "Hey I am the lookout

694 while you all eat." Splat said, "We will save you some juicy pieces. Keep an eye out

695 for old Ms. Daisy. She is a rascal." Splat said, "She is an obsolete cat and a very

696 dangerous one." MoDeep asked, "Have you seen her fangs? She can chew

697 through a monkey's tail in a cat's scratch and she's faster than grease lightning."

698 Splat explained, "She had cat charmed Olde One Claw the raven, that's how he

699 lost the claw."

700 **MoDeep said, "Yep, before he could say cat nip she cat charmed him with**

701 **those green devil cat eyes and he was frozen stiff in his track.** I saw her tip toe

702 right up on him." Lump asked, "What happened that he is still alive?" Mr. Gable

703 said, "That crazy Big Hoot crashed in kamikaze style and landed on Ms. Daisy and

704 knocked her out. She was out colder than a cold spot." Rolling laughter erupted.

705 Splat continued to laugh and said, "Hey fellas, that's pretty cold, colder than cold

706 spot 'fridgerator." rolling laugher erupted.   **Mr.**

707 **Gable said, "However, she had grabbed old Cutty Sark by the claw and those**

708 **razors in her mouth took his claw clean off. She was laying out cold with a large**

709 **claw in between her fangs."** Mr. Gable continued while laughing, "What a sight to

710 see, and let me tell you all old Cutty Sark scrambled his self up on that one good

711 claw and flip flopped, airborne.

712

Chapter VIII
Kumikaze
Crows

713   Big Hoot snapped at him as he flew past him. He reached for some sky. Last

714   I saw, Ms. Daisy was walking crazy and kind of sideways. She was still groggy from

715   that kamikaze owl crash."

716   **Splat said, "Hey lookup! It's Howie and the Winsor gang!" Lump said,**

717   **"They are headed this way and flapping fast."** MoDeep said, "Hey, heads up, they

718   are being chased by the whole Hoot Family. Scram, scram, fellas." There was an

719   explosion of black feathers and the crows scattered in all directions. Mr. Gable

720   screamed, "Rendezvous at Coon Box Fork, the West 40 of Dow Plantation, to

721   regroup!" Howie was flying like a drunken kamikaze crow. Up, down, zigzag, flips,

722   rolls, curvy loops and Big Hoot and his gang of 100 owls was hot on his tail.

723   **All this ruckus of a life and death chase began in the barn yard of Tomahawk**

724   **Farms Pigs Nest.** Howie was perched on the barn window sill; Lil Chicharon was in

725   her favorite corner of the Big Red barn next to the mud pit. Howie said, "You know

726   Lord Winsor buried the treasure on the plantation. He was being slick." 'Lil

727   Chicharon interrupted him, "What? How do you know this Howie?" Howie said,

728   "That crazy man killed 100 black slaves to protect that secret."

729

730   'Lil Chicharon said, "No one is that low down." Howie said, "Well Chicha,

731   the world is full of surprises."

732   **And at that very moment Howie didn't know Razor, son of Big Skeezer and**

733   **Naga'ena the Egyptian Cobras, were hiding in the barn wall.** Razor overheard the

734   forbidden conversation taking place between Howie and 'Lil Chicha. There was

735   also another set of eyes and ears listening to this conversation, high in the ceiling

736   wall. Eight legs spread into her web and eight eyes keenly focused on the heat

737   signature of little Razors' body.

738   **There was a sharp set of ears listening carefully at his every move and**

739   **even though they served the same ungrateful master, she is Chicha's friend.** One

740   day she might be asked by Black Fang to death bite Chicha while she sleeps or

741   maybe she should death bite Razor now. She slowly released her web gliding ever

742   so gently downwards. Quiet as death, she was in striking distance of her prey that

743   was still completely unaware of her presence. There was a loud rustling sound in

744   the wall that frightened Howie and Chicha. With more rustling and a loud hissing,

745   Chicha ran out of the barn, and Howie and the gang flew away.

Widows
encounter
with
Razor

747   **Howie said, "Caw, caw, caw meet me at Salt-Lick-Hollow by the drinking**

748   **Rock.** Caw, caw, caw." Howie swooped by Coon Box Fork to get Toot and Hatchet.

749   Howie said, "We are in trouble! They deltaed their wings in a hurry and they

750   disappear into the horizon. Meanwhile back at the feed bin, Chicha said; "O my

751   goodness, Howie and I were talking then suddenly a loud thump then two then

752   three, loud hissing. Someone or something was in the inner barn wall hiding and

753   screaming, hissing, fighting, wrestling, for its life. I wonder who it could be. It

754   sounded like…, they were dead or dying, well maybe, nah, it couldn't have been. I

755   am afraid to go back and look. Well, maybe I should go back and take a peek. Oh

756   no, what if they are still there? Then what do I do?" **The feed bin was buzzing**

757   **with excited voices asking, "What's all this Ruckus bout? And who's dead?" In**

758   **loud husky voice ask Big TOM; the blue mule?** Chicha said, "Ah, ah, ah, well ah,

759   Oh my! It, it is happened so fast. One minute we was talking and the next there

760   was this loud wrestling, banging against the inner wall, loud hissing loud

761   scrubbing against the wall, more rustling, loud hissing and we ran away as fast as

762   we could.

763

Chapter IX
Terrorism

765   **Uncle West, Chicha said, "Who's we? And where was this hissing, Ms Julia**

766 **and Uncle West" said big Tom. Sis Corine,** Chicha is rattled, Sis. Corine said "come

767   here sweetie, calm down. Relax a minute, you all upset, Ms. Corine. Hey honey!

768   Calm down, catch your breath, cool off, you're sweating up a storm, there is no

769   one chasing you right now." With that, Chicha slumped to her knees and began

770   oinking. She stretched out in the mud pit next to the Silo and said, "Ahaah that

771   feels so good, so much better." "Well, ah let me start at the beginning."

772   **Chicha said, "Oh I'm so stressed, let me see where I can begin.** I was in the

773   barn relaxing in the hay box corner by the window, when Howie landed on the

774   window sill."

775   **Ms. Corine said, "Who's Howie?"** Bre George said, "You don't know

776   Howie? Howie is Don Crow's son. Ms Corine replied "Is that crazy crow his son?"

777   "Yep, that's him." said Big Tom, and Ms. Corine said "That's a crazy crow."

778   **Chicha interrupted, "Excuse me, Excuse me, I was speaking, how rude!**

779   Anyways, Howie flew in and was telling me that I should

781 become a show pig in the 4H show this month. He also said he had a secret, He

782 and his family wanted to share with me and all of you. He wanted to know if we

783 could be trusted!" The barn yard crowds were talking among themselves in a low

784 murmur, what kind of secret?

785 **Uncle West said "Chicha is you crazy? That Howie is loony, and that gang**

786 **of hoodlums he flies with is gung ho crazy."** Big Tom said "Lil Chicha, Mrs.

787 Corine, Bre George, why in the heck are you wasting your time listening to the

788 craziest crow in Mississippi? Chicha, we hoped you would know better. You keep

789 listening to Howie and that scumbag Black Fang and his gang of twenty million

790 blood suckers along with Black Raven and his gang of criminals. Big Hoot, Black

791 Widow and her ten thousand hungry little killers are going to show up here in the

792 dark of the night and kill us all." "Shut up", said Chicha, "I was speaking, do you

793 wanna here it or not"?

794 **The crowd, which included Miss Hester, BreParker, Sis Hazel, 'Lil M.L, 'Lil**

795 **Milton, 'Lil Gussy, Sis Catherine, 'Lil Jimmy, 'Lil Bev, 'Lil Karl, Big Kinny Earl, BIG**

796 **Larry, and Poo Cat, Black Gal, 'Lil squirrel, Thresher bird were murmuring,**

797 speaking for the barn yard crowd, Uncle

799 West said "weeelllllll, Go on with your story Chicha." Chicha retold the events that

800 lead up to this moment. "I was so frightened. I am glad I found you all here. I feel

801 so much better but I, I am afraid to go back to the barn and see what happened."

802 **Uncle West said "Chicha that sounds mighty strange."**The crowd

803 murmured. "Well, well, folks what do you all think?" They continued to murmur

804 **Ms. Julia spoke for the crowd "West, you and Big Tom, Bre George you all**

805 **get on over there to that Big Red barn and see who's dead and be careful."** Bre

806 George said, "Ms Julia, y'all are talking crazy! This could be very dangerous." He

807 continued. "This is a job for Ms. Daisy and that gang of rat killers she runs with."

808 "Oh stop wining," said Lil Red, "y'all are all a bunch of Yellow Belly Chickens, and

809 I'm a Chicken." "You Tell'um Red," said Mrs. Julia. Red, "Anyways Bre George you

810 smelly old goat, whatever critter it is, your stink will knock it out." Rolling laughter

811 spread around the feed bin.

812

Chapter x
Discovery

813

814   'Lil Red said, "I am a chicken but I am not chicken hearted and I'm not

815   chicken to go, all you big talking fuddy duddys, all fradie cats. Come on Chicha,

816   let's get the heck out of here and go see what that was. I ain't got time to mess

817   with all these fuddy duddys, and scaredy cats. Y'all look after my babies till I get

818   back Ms Corine." "Ok Red!" With that said Red, Chicha and Big Tom followed

819   talking among themselves.

820   'Lil Red said, "I am getting a strange feeling." The closer she got to the barn

821   the stronger the feeling became, the feeling of being watched from a distance,

822   someone or something was watching them the feathers stood up on the back of

823   her neck, she got a tingling down her chicken spine, her eyes rolled around and

824   the little good luck charm around her neck began to vibrate. She looked up and

825   sure enough, high above, circling over head was a tiny group of out of focus dots.

826   **Distant Observers**

827   "What are those?" asked little Red looking up. "What did you say Red?"

828   asked Big Tom. "Look up; what are those dots way

829   up high?" "Yah, I see um." Uncle West, said "Oh yes, I see them."

830 **"Oh, yes I see them. Looks like crows, but they don't fly in circles", said Big Tom.**

831 "I think those maybe hawks," said Chicha.

832 **Big Tom says, "Chicken Hawk, Hawks don't do that together twenty at a**

833 **time.** It would be only one circling. Chicha looked up, her tail lost its curliness,

834 "Oh my god, it's, it's Scallywag and his gang of gutter boys." Big Tom, "I believe,

835 Chicha's right, they are circling over the barn, what ever thy spied must not be

836 dead yet they are too high in the sky. If it was dead they would be at the tree top

837 level or on the ground. They are still observing the prey." 'Lil Red said, "Hurry, let's

838 get there before they do, double time." Up the dirt path they all plotted and

839 trotted as they approached the barn. They hid beside the tractor to catch their

840 breath, and to regroup. Red said, "Big Tom, you're the strongest, go to the side

841 barn, right by the corner." Tom asked, "Ha! Chicha, which side? Right in front, just

842 beside the sycamore tree?" "Just walk by and see if you see anything. Come back

843 and tell us what you see."

844 **Big Tom said "What if there ain't nothing to see?" "Just go, hurry!"** Tom

845 began by munching on grass as he approached the barn. Munching and walking,

846 munching and walking. Didn't take long, he began munching on the sycamore

847   tree.   Sure enough he spied something he couldn't see what it was, it looked

848   familiar. What is that? He was thinking to himself, what are those colors? Where

849   have I seen those colors before?

850   **He began to eat lower on the tree to get a better look at the colors that**

851   **were glistening between the cracks in the barn outer wall.** As he drew closer, it

852   moved. He continued to munch on the tree, it moved very slowly and there was a

853   peculiar sound. A rubbing sound, like ah, ah, at that very second he suddenly

854   knew what he was seeing. It was moving strangely, not in a normal smooth,

855   sliding motion. It was jerking, why is it jerking like that? It's as though it's being

856   dragged. What, what, it's as though it is being dragged. But dragged by what?

857

858   **He stopped munching and focused his big brown eyes, as the bright**

859   **morning sunlight spread between each crack of the buckling cypress boards**

860   **along the bottom edge of the barn.** He saw a glistening leg with fine, black hair.

861   Then another and another, he dare not get any closer.

862   **He continued to munch and look, sure enough, it never saw him, it just**

863   **continued to tug at its prey and yank it.** He recognized it. It was Widow; she has

864   paralyzed or killed a member of Skeezer's family and is out weighed by his size. So

865   she's yanking and pulling him to her nest.

866   **Widow's Warning**

867   **Tom said "Widow is that you?" The yanking stopped. Widow** said "Who is

868   using my name?" "It's, it's me Tom. What happened?" Widow said, "Tom you best

869   not know my personal business. Its best you go blind than to know what

870   happened here today." Tom said, "Widow, Chicha said she was in danger here

871   earlier this morning. Did you see anything or hear anything?" Widow said, "Tom,

872   Chicha is my dearest friend and only friend. She was yakking with that crazy

Chapter XI

Oppression

873

874 Howie and didn't know she was being spied on by the Black Master's slickest

875 agent and deadliest hunter. Do you know who that is?"

876 **Tom said, "No, I don't know."** Widow said, "It's Razor, the son of Nagaena

877 and Big Skeezer." Tom said, "Widow I don't think I want to hear any more of this

878 story. Those two Black Cobras are ruthless." Widow said, "If you don't want to

879 know, don't ask. I suggest you quit munching here and go munch elsewhere or

880 you are going to see your last sight." Tom asked. "What do you mean by that?"

881 **Meanwhile, 'Lil Red and the gang were freaking out hiding behind the**

882 **tractor.** They could not hear the entire conversation with Widow, they were too

883 far away. Tom was so intent on talking with Widow that he had not noticed that

884 Big Scallywag and the Gutter Boys were also listening to Widow spill the beans on

885 herself from the tree tops.

886 **Widow said, "Tom, Master Raven is my boss, his boss is Black Fang he is**

887 **not one to be trifled with.** I am warning you. If you don't leave now you will

888 become your own worst enemy." Tom said, "I ain't scared of nothing and nobody."

889 Widow said, "Tom you sleep standing up?" Tom said."Yes, well, well, ah yea,

890   what's that got to do with anything?" Widow said, "How well can you see in the

891   dark?" Tom replied "Ah, not, not at all."

892   **Widow said, "Tom I see everything at night. I can see you two miles away**

893   **from the barn asleep under the hickory tree in the south field."** As though

894   stunned by a bolt of lightening, panic hit Tom, he galloped passed the tractor and

895   headed towards the watering pond, with 'Lil Red, Chicha, and the gang scrambling

896   to catch up with him. He was galloping so fast, 'Lil Red had to fly to keep pace

897   with him. Chicha broke into a heavy hog gallop and Uncle West had to goat pronk

898   to keep pace. When Tom got to the pond he ran straight in to the middle of the

899   pond.

900   **'Lil Red said, "What in the heck is wrong with you Tom?** You look

901   frightened!" Tom said, "Did you hear that, did you hear that? She told me I was a

902   big red lunch bag glowing in the dark. Oh my God! Oh my God! She threatened my

903   life. She said she could see me two miles away at night, glowing in the dark. That

904   hungry, black 'Lil witch told me my life is in danger if I stayed there any longer.

905   **Widow**

906   **Tom was shaking like a leaf.** Widow had frightened him to the core. Chicha

907   said,"Tom, you big fraidy cat, did you see anything? Who was there?" Tom said,

908   "It is Widow." "What was Widow doing behind that wall?" asked Chicha. Tom

909   said, "Ooooooohhh no! Ooooohhh no! I am not going to tell you nothing. I haven't

910   seen nothing, I don't know nothing." Chicha said, "Tom you big chicken, you best

911   to tell us what you saw. We are your only protection against Widow and her gang

912   of 'Lil killers." Tom said, "This pond is my insurance policy to protect me from

913   Widow. You can't do nothing to save me from that herd of 'Lil black killers she

914   carries on her back and belly." Chicha said, "Tom, spiders can walk on water." Tom

915   said, "Holy Jesus, only Jesus can do that." Chicha said, "So can spiders. This pond

916   isn't safe, but I do know one safe place." All eyes were on Chicha and hanging on

917   her every word. In a unified voice, "Where is that?" asked the crowd, in fearful

918   tones.

919   **Chicha said, "Tom, you tell us what you saw and I'll tell you how to be safe**

920   **from Widow and her 'Lil gang of killers."** Tom's eyes were rolling like giant

921   marbles in orbit. "Ah, ah, well, Chicha, Widow

Chapter XII
Subdragation

922

923 threatened me. Do you know what that means? There's no safe place." Chicha

924 said" Yes there is." Tom said, "Why did I let you monkeys talk me into this mess.

925 Give me a hint Chicha."

926 **Chicha said, "No Tom, give us the truth about what you saw Widow**

927 **doing."** There was the flapping sound of big wings landing. All eyes looked up. The

928 crowd gasped "It's, oh no! It's Big Scallywag and his gang landing in the dead tree

929 in the middle of the pond above Big Tom." You could see Tom trembling in the

930 water causing it to send out mini waves, headed to the shore.

931 **Big Scallywag and the Early Risers**

932 **Big Scallywag said, "Well, well, what do we have here?** A regular dairy

933 queen." smug laughter came from his gang. "You folks have a mule stuck in a

934 pond," More laughter from his gang. "Tom, you look might tasty standing in the

935 water all wet and juicy." There was rolling laughter from the other buzzards and

936 Tom's friends. Tom was very upset. "Chicha, why are you giggling? This isn't funny."

937 Tom was ticked off. Big Scallywag said, "Heeey fella's dripping mule sauce. We

938 can taste the sweetness" The gang laughed. "Tom you should have not messed

939 with that black witch Widow." Tom said, "Y'all get out of here, this isn't funny." Big

940 Scallywag said, "two years ago around midnight while pappy was asleep she

941 climbed up to his sleeping perch and death bit him twice, I saw her but was too

942 scared to attack her, she and her gang wrapped him in a web cocoon and

943 disappeared before daylight. We never found a single feather. My mom told us she

944 saw Widow in the moonlight glistening as she scampered down from our nest. So

945 Tom, she is on your tail." Big Tom said, "Shut up! You low life, we've heard that

946 story before."

947 **Chicha said"What story?"** Big Scallywag said "Widow killed Big Skeezer's

948 oldest son Razor. He was hiding in the wall listening to you Chicha, and that crazy

949 crow, Howie this morning" Laughter from the gang "That Howie is one crazy crow."

950 Chicha said, "How y'all know Howie was over there this morning?" Big Scallywag

951 said, "We are the early risers, Chicha, and we are the highest birds in the sky. We

952 are so high, pot, won't get us no higher. Yep, that's right" said little clucker. Nelle

953   Scallywag said, "We go down to Pot valley and get that loco weed and it just

954   makes us fly the coop, we get so high we go into Orbit" laughed old nasty

955   Scallywag. Chicha said, "This is a drug free farm and you guys aren't funny" with

956   her nose in the air. She turned her back to them to face Big Tom

957   **"Proud words for a pork rib dinner" laughed Big Scallywag.** "Hey fella's, rib

958   plate to go." Rolling laughter came from the gang. "Put me down for a pound of

959   short pork ribs with mule steaks on the side" yelled Old Bone Breaker Scallywag.

960   Big Scallywag said, "Chicha, you are in great danger. That Howie, crazy as he may

961   be, has unwittingly let Widow know that his family has the keys to the great

962   secrets of Winsor and Blue Water. Chicha said, "What are you talking about?" 'Lil

963   Scallywag whispering said, "Hey boss, maybe he didn't tell her the whole story."

964   Big Scallywag said, "Maybe not, Chicha, Howie is in deep kimpshi with the Black

965   Ballers. Widow is a member of the crew, so Chicha, don't be sleeping anywhere

966   you can be found" Rolling laughter from the gang of buzzards. "We will be having

967   Dinner over you ha ha ha." Group laughter erupted. Big Scallywag said, "Catch our

968   drift?" Raising his wings slightly and peering over the top of his wings. Chicha

969   replied "You're not having any dinner here baby! But anyway, you mean Howie's

970   family knows about Lord Winsor? What is this about Blue Water?" Big Scallywag

971   interrupted "Hey, Chicha, we got to catch us some grub. Maybe a little road kill.

972   See ya!" Loud flapping as eighty great black buzzards became airborne. A rush of

973   High Wind from the flapping of wings, up, up and away yelled Big Scallywag; as

974   swift as Bats outta hell they disappeared into the horizon. Chicha had a confused

975   look on her snout.

976   **Widow's Walk on Water**

977   **Big Tom was still standing in the pond neck deep; vibrating nervously he**

978   **created little waves from his massive mule body that went out rolling towards**

979   **the shore.** Chicha yelled, "Tom, you big fraddie cat, get out of the pond. Widow

980   can walk on water so you ain't safe. As a matter of fact, none, and I mean none of

981   us are." The crowd replied "That's bull hockey Chicha. Widow only saw Big Tom.

982   Are you guys blind? Did you not see eighty big, black winged critters fly off a few

983   minutes ago? They are loyal to their empty stomachs, and you can bet Black

984   Raven will be told about all of us by them. We are just lunch or supper for them.

985 You got that, boneheads? We have to find out the rest of this story about Blue

986 Water and Lord Winsor place and pronto or we are all lunch for the Scallywags"

987 **'Lil Red said, "Chicha, we have to find that Howie.** Where in the heck does he

988 hang out?" Chicha said, "Howie, maybe, at the elderberry trees down at the salt

989 lick. They get mighty drunk on them berries, sweet, elderberries and salt. Ok, lets

990 all see if we can track down Howie." The crowd said, "Chicha are you loco or just

991 Looney?! That Howie has wings and they been eating elderberries and salt that

992 spells drunk birds, Chicha, they could be anywhere and including passed out

993 somewhere." Chicha said, "Oh ye of little faith. Think positive, you are so negative.

994 I am positive and optimistically sure he is loud mouthing anyone at the elderberry

995 tree that has an ear. He is a social butterfly. Get a little wine in him and he is a non

996 stop talker.

997   **Salty Drunk Crows at Tutti Fruiti**

998 **The crowd said "Are you sure Chicha?"** Chicha said, "Head 'em up; move

999 'em out, rolling, rolling, rolling, raw hide." They filed behind Chicha. She headed

1000 for the Salt Lick, over the river and thru the woods on a beautiful sunlit meadow

1001   and passed through the mist rising from the blue lily covered pond. They

1002   approached the cat tails which were bobbing in the light breeze, blowing from the

1003   south. Carrying the smell of honey suckle and the sweet smell of

Chapter XIII
Transgressor

1005   elderberries. The ground was speckled with bird drippings and half processed

1006   seeds mixed with the rich smell over ripe persimmons. As they approached, Uncle

1007   West said, "Last one to the Persimmon tree is a Fig Newton." That said he did a

1008   billy goat hop, pronk and skip hopped pronked into the distance. Tom was

1009   galloping ahead and 'Lil Red flapping, hopping and flying. Chicha is full pig gallop,

1010   headed to the tree for fresh select fruit droppings, mmmmm what a treat. It was

1011   fruit heaven. The ground was a mass of yellow and green and brownish mashed

1012   and squished over ripe fruit. Uncle Billy had reared up on his hind legs to get the

1013   freshest and best ripe fruit from the tree. This prompted Chicha to do the same

1014   and Tom just raised his large powerful head and plucked juicy fresh fruit from the

1015   low hanging limbs. As they were becoming tutti frutti, they failed to notice they

1016   were being watched and very keenly by a flock of mag pies.

Trespass at Tutti Fruitti Orchard

1018   **Maggie Mag said, in a shrill voice, "Hello, Hello, what do you think?** And

1019   who do you guys think you are? How rude, this is private property and this is our

1020   tree. Get outta here!" She was furious. She

1021

1022   was also being ignored by all. She might as well be talking to herself. Chicha and

1023   crew were starved and tuned her out. Mad Maggie squawked," enemy allies

1024   tennn, tennn, tennn" a call for all birds (911 help). Maggie was not one to be

1025   ignored she began dive attacking the largest member that was Big Tom, who first

1026   ignored Mad Maggie. Tom was darting his head back and forth until he began

1027   using his tail as a bird swatter. He slapped Mad Maggie silly with a powerful tail

1028   swipe. Mad Maggie was screaming very loud. It caught the attention of the crowd

1029   at the Salt Lick, a stones throw away from the Persimmon Trees.

1030   **Maggie squawked out a sound recognized by all the birds, including the**

1031   **most notorious crows.** Howie and the gang fired up their most murderous of

1032   squawk and dive bombers and within seconds they were airborne. They headed

1033   for the Persimmon Tree. There were robbers and invaders to drive away. Howie,

1034   managed to get some altitude. He flung himself in the heavens skyward, then he

1035   and his companion each spin rolled, arched their wings and rolled into a dive.

1036   Howie had selected a large pinkish target in the group of Maggie's invaders and

1037   aimed his attack straight for its head.

1038

1039

1040 Streaking towards his target, he could hear the wind whistling pass his ears, faster

1041 and faster, wait there is something familiar about this target. What? The distance

1042 was closing very fast that hat with a single, yellow flower.

1043 **Howie said, "Holy pig snout, it's, it's Chicha."** He rolled left, then, reverse

1044 flip, slam, bang, pow an explosion of black feathers, dead into Mad Maggie and

1045 her two companions, all knocked out cold. Chicha said: "Oh my, holy cat scratch,

1046 Howie is dead! Howie, speak to me! Howie, Howie, wake up!" Chicha lifted him

1047 gently in her mouth and shook him. He was limp as a dead cat. All the locals and

1048 his gang, Mad Maggie's friends were nudging Maggie and Media and Loot to see if

1049 they were dead. Suddenly Chicha snatched Howie from the ground and streaked

1050 into a pigs gallop headed for the Salt Lick and babbling brook at high speed.

1051 Everyone was stunned at her quickness.

1052 **Zoom, zoom, quicker than a pig's snout.** She laid Howie down at the waters

1053 edge. She dipped her mouth into the water, took a large mouthful of water and

1054 sprayed Howie. Gasping and choking and flapping and kicking, Howie sprung to

1055 life. "What, what the heck happened?" Chicha spun around and zoom, zoom quick

1056 as a flash she picked up Mad Maggie and Loot and Media and zoom, zoom, back

Chapter XIV
Trespassers
&
A Pig Hissy

1057   to the Water's Edge, where Howie was still staggering around like a drunken bird.

1058   Chicha sucked up a large mouth of water and sprayed Loot, Mida, and Maggie.

1059   They all sputtered and flapped and chucked, coughing back to life. Each looked

1060   bewildered in shock. "What the what, who, hit me?" squawked Maggie,

1061   "something hit me like a brick wall. Loot, who, what's going on? Where am I? Who

1062   are all of you? Media, oh my, holy cheese and crackers. Someone ran over me.

1063   Where am I and what are all you critters looking at me like I was dead or

1064   something?"

1065   **The crowd murmured**. Chicha said" Y'all got hit by a whatie?" Uncle West

1066   said "By a Kamikaze! Crow! And y'all looks to be undead, he, he, he. Crowd rolling

1067   with laughter. Mad Maggie, shuttering and fluffing her feathers and puffing out

1068   her breast said "You Big Tom? Mr. West. Lil Red, what's nerve you have invading

1069   my Persimmon tree." (Crowded Murmur) 'Lil Red, "Excuse us, this tree ain't got

1070   your name anywhere on it." Mad Maggie said, "This land is Blue Water Plantation,

1071   owned by Lord Chamberlain, may he rest in peace and Lord John Nobel. Are you

1072   smarting off at the mouth? For your information miss smarty feathers," her yellow

1073   beak snapping with anger "Let me clean up any blind spots. My family has been

1074 nesting here for one thousand years. Long before any two legged bald headed

1075 humans showed up to plant a single crop on this land. This tree is my family

1076 nesting place. If you all don't show some respect, we are gonna peck your eyes

1077 down to the nub. You got that shortie! Maggie said," Red I don't care for your

1078 kind. Anyhow, you banny roosters and hens have a bad reputation for being

1079 fighting cocks. I know your family history, you best shut up." Chicha said, "Wait a

1080 minute Maggie! There's a misunderstanding. We didn't come here to steal your

1081 fruit or invade your home. Uncle West and Big Tom sure didn't either." Uncle West

1082 said, "You tell her Chicha." Chicha, "We came here to find Howie." Mad Maggie

1083 said, "It looks like you got more than you bargained for, and you found this

1084 reckless flying dodo" shaking a balled up wing fist at Howie. Mad Maggie said,

1085 "Howie this is restricted air space. I have babies living here. You best slow down."

1086 Howie said, "You ungrateful witch we were flying to rescue you." Epiphany,

1087 Howie's sister knew what was on Chicha's mind. She interrupted Chicha,

1088

1089 "Howie, we best be headed home. Big daddy has a family meeting planned in a

1090 few minutes. Let's skedaddle before we get in big trouble." Chicha, "Excuse me,

1091 hello! I was speaking." Epiphany said, "Come on Howie, right now, or Big Daddy's

1092 gonna pluck us alive. I meant it. I am leaving." Like a black rocket, she flung

1093 herself skyward, leaving a single black feather swirling in mid air. "I am gonna tell

1094 Howie, if you don't scram right now." Howie looked confused. "I gotta go Chicha.

1095 Big Daddy will pop pluck me alive. "With a deep breath he flung himself into the

1096 blue sky and disappeared with his crew, squawking among themselves. Chicha

1097 said, "Wait, wait, Howie! Don't leave Howie!" Howie said, "I see you tomorrow,"

1098 his voice fading in the wind.

1099 **Chicha's Pig Hissy**

1100 Chicha, very upset, stamped around in a pig frenzy snorting, flinging dust,

1101 kicking, hopping up and down, and rolling around in the dust. It was such

1102 outrageous behavior for her, it frightened her friends. Lil Red said, "Chicha, stop it.

1103 Stop it right now! What is wrong with you?" Big Tom took five or six steps away

1104 from Chicha. Uncle West stepped back and lowered his horns to push her away

1105 from him.

1106

1107   Lil Red hopped on Uncle West horns. He was yelling, "Stop it! Stop Chicha!"

1108   Chicha flung herself into the ground, rolled on her back, kicking her legs in mid air,

1109   oinking and squealing loud in frustration. Big Tom walked over to the water,

1110   sucked up a big mouth, aimed it at Chicha and sprayed her head with a loud

1111   splash. Chicha flopped flat on the ground with a thud. Big Tom said, "Cool off,

1112   Chicha! Cool off!" Chicha's big ears hanging over her eyes hid the blue outer rings

1113   of her eye that was full of tears. Big water tears, flowing like a waterfall. Chicha

1114   said, "We, sob, came, sobbing, all this way, sobbing, to find sobbing, Howie and

1115   that insensitive Lil Winch, sister of his. She is so controlling. She gets on my last

1116   nerve. Every time she is visiting me at the barn, she interrupts our visit. We gotta

1117   go, we gotta go," mocking epiphany in a high pitch voice. "I can't stand her. She is

1118   a royal pain in the neck." Sobbing, nose running, "I could just squeeze her 'lil

1119   claws off." 'Lil Red: "Well, let's go eat persimmons and go home." "Yeah," said

1120   Uncle West. Big Tom, "yeah, persimmons sound good."

1121   They waited on Chicha to get to her feet and walked towards the

1122   persimmons tree. 'Lil Red was standing on Uncle West head

Chapter XV
Homeward Bound

1124 between his horns. The sun was slowly sinking into the Western sky with

1125 scattered clouds turning the southern sky into a multicolored spectrum of orange,

1126 blues and pastel reds. 'Lil Red said, "Wow! Look at that sunset! Oh yeah! Hurry

1127 up, we gotta get home. Eat up fellas." The persimmons were at peak ripeness.

1128 They had reached the bright yellow, soft, mushy melt in your mouth, stage. Each

1129 morsel was sweet and juicy. "Um, um," said Uncle West, "this is a wonderful treat,

1130 Red." Red was smacking her beak on a large plump one. Chicha had stopped

1131 sobbing and began happy oinking and got back to her chipper self. Big Tom said,

1132 "Oh, I'm stuffed. It's getting late. We best to mosie towards the farm." With that

1133 said they all nibbled here and there at fallen fruit and moved homeward. Big Tom

1134 lead and Uncle West following. 'Lil Red riding his back and Chicha tailing last, ears

1135 flopping quietly headed home. They arrived over the river and through the woods

1136 at the Big Red Barn. 'Lil Red said, "Goodnight Big Tom and Uncle West." Lil Red

1137 hopped to Chicha's back from Uncle West back, "See y'all tomorrow." Chicha

1138 headed down with Lil Red riding her upper shoulder. Lil Red said, "Hey Chicha, I

1139 don't think it's a good idea to have so many ears around

1140

THE LEGEND OF BLUE WATER TREASURE
AT
Winsor Ruins

Author Parker Chamberlain
Illustrator Parker Chamberlain

Published by:
Publisher number:

Episode III

President Barack Obama

"As we began the 21st century, education is first. For no child to be left behind is paramount, head start to college. Step up."

Chapter XVI
Loud Mouth Loon

1141 when you speak to Howie. I think that's why his sister was afraid of what he was

1142 going to tell you, or what you were going to ask him about Blue Water." "Not

1143 much, except it can get you hurt real bad and this secret is three hundred years

1144 old. That crazy gal Loon has been trying to find Lord Winsor's Treasure for a long

1145 time." Chicha said, "I am surprised you know this. How did you find out about

1146 Loon?" "Chicha, you forget Loon and Winkey and old Mann feed us every morning

1147 and she is a regular chatterbox. She is always scheming to find treasure. That

1148 Loon is a real corker." Chicha, "Loon is my dearest friend." "You think I don't know

1149 that Chicha? Well I do. I also know that Howie's sister Epiphany knows that also.

1150 She sits outside Loons window and listens at everything she can hear. At night we

1151 spotted the murderous white owl and his gang of killers, listening at her window

1152 also because Loon has a big mouth."

Loud Mouth Loon

1154 "She talks too much and spills the beans on everybody. Chicha, before you

1155 get too deep over your head, you need to consider who will get hurt if loud mouth

1156 Loon is overheard by the wrong ears. You also Chicha, are at risk, these protectors

1157 of the secrets are real and

1159   dangerous. Before you risk your life and the others who share secrets with you,

1160   you need to think clearly about the end result. If she is successful, who benefits

1161   and who loses in the end? Loon goes home and we are stuck here to pay

1162   whatever price the protectors choose to raid upon us. That includes you Chicha.

1163   Well we are here at my place." Red's chicks ran over to gather around her,

1164   chirping. Chicha, "You know Red, I never thought about helping me look closer at

1165   my actions and my choice of words of cause and effects. You think Loon would

1166   take us away form here, if she found the treasure?" Red, "Chicha this is my home.

1167   I don't want to leave home. I have family to take care of. You only have you. You

1168   need to look at everyone that you have contact with and what the effect of your

1169   actions will cause to happen in each of our lives. Those protectors are killers.

1170   They mean business. Life is about choices. We have to choose what the best path

1171   is for our lives. Wrong choices have a broad scope of effect on everyone you know.

1172   So choose wisely Chicha." Lil Red, "When you see Howie you may not want to

1173   know what he is carrying. It is his family curse. Do you need anymore pain like

1174   you were feeling at the Salt Lick? That was a tiny

Talk too much to many ears many listening

1176 bit of pain. Imagine much more when he tells you the whole truth and his little

1177 sister tells Big Daddy that Howie has spilled the family beans. What if Looney

1178 Loon slips and Old Hootie Owl and black Raven find out you know their weakness

1179 and secrets? What and where will you hide?" "Oh no! I didn't think about that

1180 Red. Say it one more time. I didn't think about that Red." "You better get a good

1181 night sleep Chicha." Red gathered her little ones and headed for the coop,

1182 chirping and chattering in the nest. Chicha strolled toward the farm house to lie

1183 under Loon's room and listen to what she might hear and to think about her

1184 conversation with Red. She was very frightened about making the wrong choice.

1185 Lying under Loon's room, would help her learn more about Loon and her way, can

1186 she be trusted with the safety of others and keep a secret. She will observe Loon

1187 for the next month or so to see if her actions prove she is the correct choice, to

1188 share the secret of Blue Water. Chicha arrived at the house. She crossed the back

1189 gate and squealed. You know and I know, the two blue tick hounds. They looked

1190 at her and eased out from under the house to the edge of the front steps. Then

1191 they lay down to finish their nap. Chicha scratched up a little dust pad and

Chapter XVII
Bad Dreams

1193 lay down under Loon's room to rest for the night. She could hear Loon chattering

1194 away on the telephone to her friend Liza. Winkey was teasing Loon about her

1195 loud mouth and poking fun at Liza about what happened at the Sunday School

1196 Barbecue. Loon was laughing at Liza getting potato salad slung all over her new

1197 summer dress.

1198   **Looney Loon**

1199   They were talking about someone named Suzie Q. being a boyfriend stealer.

1200 Chicha's eyes were very heavy; she slowly drifted in a deep sleep. The edge of a,

1201 a, a, dream. "Oh my! What's happening? Look, please don't hurt me. Oh, oh, oh.

1202 long night." There were bad dreams. It was as though Lil Red's word came to life.

1203 Chicha was being chased. She was running full gallop and her heart was pounding

1204 like thunder, she glanced over her shoulder, "Oh No", it's Black Raven, Big Hootie

1205 Owl, Big Skeezer, sharp teeth Miss Daisy. Black Widow and hundreds of her 'lil

1206 killers, and Black Eagle, were hot on her trail chasing her across the Big Black

1207 Bridge, towards Blue Water Fall at lovers leap, "Oh my! Oh my! Someone help me!

1208 Help me!" She was galloping down thru the rocks over the meadow and up thru

1209 the

1210 Slave Cemetery. Around the Black Dwarf and into the babbling Brook, screaming

1211 loud. She could hear all of them. We have you now Chicha! You won't get away.

1212 She splashed faster and faster following Babbling Brook. She could hear the roar of

1213 the Blue Water Fall in the distance. The current was swift and swept Chicha off

1214 her feet. She was scrambling to head for the river shore. It's very hard to swim. I

1215 can't get my feet to get a grip on these slippery rocks. "Oh no! The water fall!

1216 Help! Help!" Over the falls, falling, falling, falling, oinking she awoke with a

1217 startled jump and squealed "IEEEE", loud and long frightening You Know and I

1218 Know the two hounds to trembling wide-eyed, awake, they were staring at Chicha

1219 from across the yard, tails curled, hair bristled on their backs, sniggling at Chicha,

1220 "Ah huh", yup said You Know, I've had a few of those kinds of dreams",

1221 me too, said I Know. The first day I saw your face Chicha, I was scared to go to

1222 sleep, they both howled with laughter eyeballing her as she banged her head on

1223 the flooring rafters. "What? What?" She was safe under the farmhouse. Chicha

1224 said, "you two dung balls are not funny!" "Oh my! What a bad dream." She

1225 managed to calm herself, realizing it was a dream. She began to realize what

1226 could go wrong when dealing with Howie's family curse. All the fear that 'Lil Red

1227 had expressed had manifested itself into a dream. Chicha was laying there

1228 thinking. When she heard Loon chatting with her friend Liz on the phone about

1229 treasure hunting and how Liz could bring some of the students from archeology

1230 class to the farm to look for Lord Winsor's Gold. Chicha also noticed the tree

1231 outside. Loon's window had two visitors perched on high limbs gathering

1232 information. Chicha looked at the fence. Hanging in the same tree, Black Widow's

1233 'lil killers were hanging beneath the leaves from the bottom up. On the roof of

1234 the farm house 'Lil Buz and Big Buz buzzards were perched, all listening to Looney

1235 Loon. Chicha thinking to herself, now I see, Loon is the wrong human to trust.

1236 Chicha pointed her pretty red polished 'lil hoofs home and stopped by 'lil Reds,

1237 then spotted her at the Silo. She told Red she had a bad dream and to confirm,

1238 Loon was too yakie and couldn't be trusted with their safety. Lil Red looked at

1239 Chicha and stretched an arrow in the dirt pointing out of the silo door, opposite

1240 the feeding area and away from the breakfast crowd. Chicha strolled casually out

1241 of the barn and to the middle of the barnyard where there was no wall. No other

1242 critters near, except her and Lil Red. She looked up and around. Then spoke in a

1243 low whisper, "Look in the pecan tree, over the barn, at the very top limbs, almost

1244 out of sight, what do you see? Focus on the tree. What is that? It's something big

1245 and winged and black with a gray spot."

1246

1247

Chapter XVIII
I-Spys
Suppression

1250   "Chicha, that's ah, ah, my goodness, it's Halo! What is he doing up there?"

1251   Chicha, "He is spying, (in a low whisper voice.) You know Red; you are one smart

1252   Lil chic. These sneaky protectors have been quietly spying on all of us for years. I

1253   never noticed till you opened my eyes last night. I am shocked." Chicha, "Old

1254   Blood Thirsty and her black brood have been hanging in the silo for years, listening

1255   in on our conversations. Every night they report to their evil lord everything we

1256   talk about." A large shadow passed over them, Chicha froze, "Oh my, lets split

1257   Red." 'Lil Red Pecks here way into the Silo. She could see Chicha headed to the

1258   corn sargum bin. Chicha began happily munching the sweet protein rich buffet as

1259   the sun disappeared into the night. The horizon lightens in soft pale blue and red

1260   then slowly bright yellow. Beautiful morning began as the night slipped into

1261   morning. Red noticed Chicha was eating alone and being antisocial. Red said,

1262   "Chicha? What, who's that?" "Oh! Red, don't sneak up on me like that." Lil Red,

1263   "Why are you so jumpy?" "Oh, who me? I'm not jumpy." "You're not being

1264   sociable today. You're over here eating by yourself. What's up? What happened

1265   to

1267 cause you to hide out eating alone?" Chicha was silent as Red asked a dozen

1268 questions. Red, "Something happened last night. Chicha, tell me what happened?

1269 You've never been antisocial. What has caused you to withdraw from the

1270 neighbors? Are you angry with me because of what I said to you about Howie

1271 yesterday?"

1272   "Forget what I said, I didn't mean to upset you." Chicha turned around to

1273 face 'lil Red and scratched the ground with her right hoof to get Red to come a

1274 little closer. Chicha looked up to the top of the Silo and back at Lil Red. Lil Red

1275 looked up to the top of the Silo and saw Old Blood Thirsty and her Black Brood

1276 hanging upside down, ears listening. Chicha said, "Good morning everyone"

1277 (crowd murmur). "Morning, Chicha." Chirps, caws and moos, cackles, maa's and

1278 whinnies and bleats from the breakfast crowd munching at the feed stalls around

1279 the Silo. Chicha drifted into the Silo to avoid any questions from the group about

1280 yesterday. She has become aware of the spy's hanging out in the trees above

1281 quietly listening to everyone, but not being noticed, very sneaky habits. Chicha

1282 has decided to see how long they have been spying on everyone and the skill and

1283 techniques and tactics, being used this is her project for the next month. She will

1284 figure out how to counter spy on the spies. She is going to need help and must be

1285 careful who she selects. It must be done in an unobserved and strict privacy.

Chapter XIX
Careful Choices

Careful Choices

1287   Chicha has to select an ally that has wings and is trustworthy and powerful.

1288   Who can that be? Let me contemplate this. Maggie said, "Good morning Chicha."

1289   "Ah, ah, good morning Maggie" said Chicha. Chicha was quiet. "What, no

1290   conversation about yesterday about Howie?" said Maggie. Chicha stopped and

1291   looked up at Maggie. Just above Maggie in the same tree perched was Halo, Black

1292   Ravens fourth son. "I don't know what your talking about Maggie, I have better

1293   things on my mind", and trotted away, nose in the air. Halfway to the feedlot,

1294   Chicha noticed, Halo had flown ahead of her and landed in the Pecan tree over the

1295   feedlot, she could hear all of the ruckus and conversation from the others as they

1296   rummaged through the grain bin munching and grunting. Uncle West, Big Tom

1297   and Lil Red and her chicks, Uncle Billy, Mrs. Corine, Miss Julia, Big Dan and Lil Dan

1298   and Ms. Holly, the field mouse and all of the swallow tails, Big Red the Red Bird

1299   and all of her family. Robbie Robbin and the crew Nat and Nan squirrel. Hip Hop

1300   the pack rat and his wife Nugget, Mr. and Mrs. Blue, the jaybirds and the entire

1301   Billy Crow family busy sorting, sifting through the seeds in the feed bin, a loud

1302   ruckus of chattering, chirps, snips and parents, teaching their young how to sort

1303   seed and grain. Chicha thinking to herself, no more open discussions with any

1304   critter regarding Blue Water and for now, Howie is off limits till I can figure out

1305 who I can trust. I will not meet Howie today anywhere. It is too dangerous.

1306 Maybe I can send him a message by his sister. No, it's too risky. I'll think about it

1307 for awhile, the day slipped into the night sky and Chicha fell asleep under Loon's

1308 room as Loon chattered on the phone.

1309 **Salty Drunk Crows**

1310   Chicha noticed the sun was breaking the Horizon. The bright yellow and

1311 blue morning clouds were parting and the sun rays were rising. Chicha rose up

1312 and stretched her back and arched her long slender body. Chicha thought it was

1313 time to wash her face and cleanup for the day; she headed for the babbling brook.

1314 Upon arrival she began splashing fresh water everywhere till she was dripping

1315 clean. "Wow that feels great!" High in the tree over the brook was Mad Maggie.

1316 She said, "Good morning Chicha." "Ah oh", good morning Maggie, said Chicha,

1317 Maggie said, what? No conversation about yesterday about Howie? Chicha

1318 stopped and looked up at Maggie, and Chicha said,

1319

1320   "good morning to you Maggie." "Feels good to be clean?" "Yes, it does, now its

1321   breakfast time and I am headed for the feed lot. See you later." She trotted up

1322   the meadow across the barn yard toward the Silo, she could hear the breakfast

1323   crowd murmuring as she drew closer. Chicha thinking to herself, "Last night I

1324   realized that some humans appear to be a good friend until you look and listen

1325   with an open mind. Then you listen from a distance to gather more about their

1326   personality. You will know whether they are busy bodies, or quite intelligent, or

1327   just shallow. Chicha saw 'Lil Red standing by the silo, she approached Red and

1328   said, "Red you have sharpened my observation skills about my so called friend.

1329   She is no friend, on closer observation Loon is shallow and greedy and a loud

1330   mouth. Loon is a poor choice for sharing any secret. However, I have heard very

1331   little from Old Mann. He has a quiet and reserved manner. He speaks very little.

1332   He may be Loons pawn. That may be a poor choice also. I need to consider all

1333   facets of this before I risk any one of the humans to trust with this secret." Chicha

1334   began to notice that the Black Master had all of his 'Lil Servants busy gathering

1335   and listening to everyone and all the critters on Tomahawk Farms and the eight or

1336   so surrounding farms. Chicha's dream had awakened her to how sneaky these

1337   protectors of the

1338

Chapter XX
Blind Deaf and Mute
Subversion

1339 treasure were, and to what lengths they would go to keep it a secret. I noticed this

1340 morning when I woke up under the Main House, under Loon's bedroom, there

1341 were sneaky spies in the white oak. They were hanging out middle of the tree

1342 where the leaves are thick and they could not be seen, the sneaky of sneaks. 'Lil

1343 Red said, "Who was it Chicha?" Chicha said, "Nagaena and Dagger." Lil Red said

1344 "Oh my goodness, the two black Egyptian cobras, what were they doing." Chicha

1345 said, "listening at Loons conversations to Liz?" "Her school mate, she was inviting

1346 her to visit to help search for Lord Windsor's Treasure. Liz is an archeologist. You

1347 know what that is Red?" 'Lil Red said, "Yeah, real trouble for all of us." Chicha,

1348 "They heard every word she had to say and then some. Red said, "I no longer feel

1349 safe in my world."

Blind Eyes, Deaf Ears, Mute Mouths

1350

1351 The protectors are everywhere. You cannot speak your mind safely ever

1352 again unless you risk being silenced forever. By this group of hide in plain sight

1353 sneak of the sneaks who make up the group of body snatchers, for Black Fang.

1354 Chicha, "Red, we can no longer speak in any place except in wide open spaces

1355 with no trees or birds overhead or flappers of any kind. It seems you and I have to

1356 find us a winged acomplis big and strong, powerful and brilliant with intelligence."

1357 Red Began strutting around in circles. Her back arched chest was sticking out, that

1358 would be me 'Lil Red, poking out of her chicken breast. "I am ready. Choose me,

1359 hee, hee, hee. All of those things you spoke are me, me, me defined." Chicha,

1360 "Stop Red, this is serious." Red's chest dropped and she unfluffed her feathers. She

1361 went back to her normal looking self, yet quiet multicolored rich looking. "'Lil Red,

1362 wide open spaces. No one can hide or sneak up on us, using sneaky peat." 'Lil

1363 Red, "Chicha, what is a sneaky peat?" "Oh, Red, you don't know what a sneaky

1364 peat is?" 'Lil Red, "No, Chicha!" Red looked up, "What don't you see, uuh uh rain,

1365 the sun, stars, the moon. Ok, I give up, what?" Chicha, "Nothing circling

1366 overhead." "Oh, I get it. They watch from on high and then when you're not

1367 lookin, they swoop down and listen and you never know they are there." "Corecta

1368 mundo, sneaky peat." 'Lil Red, "You know Chicha; I have had blinders on for a long

1369 time since you mentioned sneaky peat. These protectors have been hanging

1370 around a very long time even when my grand maw and grand paw were around.

1371 Chicha, I can remember many times and places seeing them always on the very

1372 top branches of trees, power lines roof top buildings, just about everywhere.

1373 They never interact with anyone or make conversation. Usually they are just

1374 sitting quietly, listening to everyone and looking on at a distance at everyone."

1375 Chicha said, "That's the point Red. They never interacted, strictly observational

1376 and listening in pairs. You don't even know they are above you or listening at

1377 every conversation quietly, yet blending with the surroundings." Red said, "So

1378 what do we use our new found observation for?" Chicha said, "You and I need to

1379 spy on the spies from a distance to see who they are and what their vulnerabilities

1380 are." Red said, "What is a varn-nirability?" Chicha, "Weakness, your home,

1381 children, feeding ground, family, close friends, things like that." Red said, "Chicha

1382 that's too much work, besides we can't fly that far. Oh, he-he, Oh, you're right.

1383 Well, I guess we need a better plan, something simple." 'Lil Red, "Wouldn't it be

1384 easier if we exposed them to everyone so they can't be invisible anymore? Now

1385 when they are around, everyone will heckle them. They'll say, good morning, Big

1386 Skeezer or Nagaena how are you? What's going on? You're just going to hang up

1387 there?" Chicha said, "You know Red, that's it! Destroy their invisibility. See if they

1388 fly away by intimidation. Remember be careful, you don't know how they will

1389 react." 'Lil Red said, "If everyone is doing it, they

1390

1391 won't attack the whole crowd. That would be Looney. They would be torn to bits,

1392 more of us than them. Remember, the whole crowd has to acknowledge their

1393 presence. This is the key to making them visible." Chicha, "Their spying days are

1394 numbered. The more we know about what's going on, this will disappear. We will

1395 get our privacy back." 'Lil Red, "We have to spread this around the farm and all

1396 the neighbors howl farms. Who's the loudest mouth we know?" They both speak

1397 at once, "Howie and Mad Maggie and Buzy Buzzards. No, no, they are two faced."

1398 Chicha, "Howie's not two faced, 'Lil Red, he is my friend." 'Lil Red, "Not Howie,

1399 Buzzy Buzzards and his gang are two faced." Chicha, "Ha, you mean four faced and

1400 when starved! Forty faced they eat their own mother." 'Lil Red, "Ok, ok were

1401 gonna need more than Mad Maggie and Howie." Chicha, "I don't think so. You

1402 know Howie has 350,000 family members on Tomahawk and the 5 surrounding

1403 farms and Mad Maggie at least 250,000 family and friends, she and Howie are

1404 both head of the clans." 'Lil Red, "Ah ah. What is a clan?" "Howie is the Head

1405 crow and Mad Maggie head Mag pie." "Ok, oh I get it. Wow, Chicha with these

1406 two we covered the four surrounding counties and then some, so tomorrow.

1407 Chicha you put out a call for Howie and Mad Maggie." Chicha, "No." 'Lil Red,

1408 "What, I am convinced Chicha, why not put out a call for those two?" Chicha,

1409 "This must be done quietly, or we are snake meat." 'Lil Red, "So what's your plan

Chapter XXI
The Mobbing
of
Roseta

1410 Chicha?" Chicha, "Howie and his gang are always down at the Salt Lick, drinking

1411 and eating elderberries." 'Lil Red, "Yeah and most likely drunk." Chicha, "Bad idea.

1412 'Lil Red: a drunken cow is dead crow around here and Maggie likes them

1413 Elderberry's also she most likely will be as drunk as Howie." "Chicha maybe we

1414 should find some others." Chicha, "No, no, no these two are perfect. Drunk or

1415 not Howie has excellent skills in communication and upside down flight and so

1416 does Mad Maggie if I get to Howie by 10 am he'll have spread the word by sun

1417 down and Mad Maggie by the next day we are good to go." 'Lil Red stammered,

1418 "Good to aah g-go, yeah they slapped wing to knuckle high five. Gggggooooo to

1419 ahah ggoo."

1420 **The Mobbing of Roseta**

1421   The morning air was heavy with mist, rising from the blue grass meadow on

1422 Tomahawk Farm; all the critters were buzzing and chirping. The forest was alive

1423 with newborns. Mrs. Blue J and Reddy Red bird were busy feeding her nestling

1424 fresh worms from the brook, the meandering stream that flows throughout the

1425 valley green of meadows. The brook provides fresh water for all the critters in the

1426 valley, but as we take a closer look, ah, there's Cassy coyote and six pups. Muffin,

1427 Mattie, Mongunl, Moser, Scate and Coot are all playing in the brook, splashing

1428 water all over each other. Further up the stream, Senora fox was playing with her

1429 nephews, three fox pups. They were pouncing and splashing in the brook.

1430 Punch, Jab and Stick were spitting images of their father Poncho Fox, they were

1431 being watched over by Senora Fox, Poncho's sister.

1432   She was babysitting for Roseta Fox, Poncho's beloved wife. Who went

1433 hunting for grouse bright and early that morning? She was crawling sly as a fox in

1434 the tall grass at Corn Valley at the edge of Coon Box Fork Sky way. She could see

1435 the sky monsters run on the path and leap into the sky. Their smoke filled the air.

1436 Roseta was within striking distance of a Penny Grouse. SWOOSH "Gotcha" Swift as

1437 a flash of lighting, Roseta had her for breakfast. She dispensed Penny Grouse,

1438 then laid her down and crouched into the grass to capture Perry Grouse. Quiet as

1439 death, SWOOSH "Gotcha" she dispensed Perry.

1440

1441   Roseta was unaware she was being watched by high flying Hunters, and she

1442   is on their menu. Big Hoots gang; suddenly out of the blue, as Roseta was trotting

1443   down the culvert at Coon Box Fork, she was carrying her two grouses home to

1444   feed the family. "BANG" She was slammed head first into the stone path by Big

1445   Hoots, at high speed then"BANG" another slam by 'lil'Hoots, knocking her grouse

1446   catch all over the stone path. Roseta screamed loudly "Get away from me! Woof

1447   Woof Woof" Scrambling to her feet, she was severely wounded, slipping into

1448   shock; Gray Hoots, scooped up Penny Grouse and swallowed her whole. Banti

1449   Hoots scooped Perry Grouse up and split him with 'lil' Hoots, growling at each

1450   other and gobbled him down in mid flight. They rolled and pitched at high speed

1451   and dived on Roseta's back, clawing her to the bone. Big Hoot landed behind

1452   Roseta's neck, locking his talons into her spine and paralyzing Roseta's left side.

1453   She yelped, rolled to dislodge Big Hoots, but he held fast. Lil' Hoots locked on

1454   talons into her middle spine, and then Big Gray Hoot locked talons in her neck.

1455   She was yelping, rolling, hopping, and dragging then in frantic to get away. She

1456   fled into the culvert up the hill and into the stone path of the four

Chapter XXII
Snacking

Pencils on the Meadow

1458   wheelers. SWOOSH, she heard the sound of squealing tires, then everything went

1459   black, BUMP BUMP BUMP. The owls went wild with laughter. Big Hoots said,

1460   "WOW! Did you see that? Gee wiz." Lil 'Hoots said, "She sure got smacked by

1461   that 14 wheel monster, Holy cheese and cracker!" Big Gray Hoots said, "Lucky we

1462   let go huh!" "Just in time," said BANDI, chuckling out loud. "Well Pop's," said 'Lil

1463   Hoot, "We gonna feast?" "OK," said Old Gray. "Let's grab her. One, two, three, go."

1464   They swooped down and dragged Roseta's carcass to the far side of the stone path

1465   out to the edge of the storm drain, where they feasted on her, leaving only her big

1466   red fuzzy tail at the edge of the drainage ditch. The owls were unaware they were

1467   being observed from afar by a lone traveler. Lil'Red, who was afraid to be seen,

1468   was horrified at the sight of the mobbing of Roseta. In fear she flew away swiftly

1469   and quietly as possible. Unaware that she was spotted by Big Gray Hoots.

1470   **DR.CRANE ADVISES PONCHO**

1471   Meanwhile across the meadow in deep lush grass, unaware of his loved

1472   one's peril, someone else was enjoying summer, pouncing from spot to spot. He

1473   could be seen pouncing quite a distance,

DR. CRANE; REMINDS; PANIC

1474

1475   hunting grasshoppers as snacks. Dr. Crane, "Hello, there." Poncho fox didn't

1476   respond to the call, he continued to pounce until he was directly under the voice

1477   calling him. He made a heroic leap and snagged the branch. This voice was sitting

1478   just out of reach. "Wow Poncho that was close but not close enough," laughed Dr.

1479   Crane. "Dr." said Poncho "I have delivered 118 of your family members and my

1480   father before me delivered your grand parents and none of us have been eaten.

1481   You know why Poncho, because we taste like poo times two. So thank your lucky

1482   stars you have never got a bite of me," he laughed. "Oh, Ah, by the way I stopped

1483   to let you know that 'Lil Punch Fox is gonna be just fine. I set his right paw in a

1484   splint so he can hop around, tell him stay off that free highway thing because

1485   them road 4 wheel devils don't stop for nothing except them two legged vermin

1486   called humans. So keep 'Lil Coot at home for awhile." Dr. Crane was about to fly

1487   away to his next stop, when Poncho Fox said, "Oh by the way. Dr. Crane you have a

1488   good day and my great grand daddy said you all taste like chicken." Dr. Crane

1489   looked over the rim of his glasses with a piercing look, and then soared into the

1490   late afternoon air grumbling to himself, "Dirt ball low down sneaky, I always

1491   wondered what happened to Great Great Grand Pappy." Flopped into the forest,

1492   DA-SHA-VOO-AT LOVERS LEEP. Poncho lost interest in snacking. His mind turned

1493   to home he began plodding in that direction.

Chapter XXIII
Déjà Vu

Poncho's Déjà Vu

1495   He could see lovers leap from the center of the Meadow. It was a high

1496   point over looking the Mighty Mississippi River. He could not resist a climb, on

1497   ward he pushed across the Meadow up, up, up the tri level mound. He was

1498   gasping for breath. Poncho said, "What a climb, whew, whoa Nelly and what a

1499   spectacular view." At that very second a deep fear ran over Poncho as he got

1500   closer to the edge of the hill his nose picked up the stench of death. He could

1501   hear the water fall thrashing below and see the giant clouds of splashing mist.

1502   Poncho edged closer to the down side of Lovers Leap and he could see a large

1503   dark hole. He could hear whispering of some kind but he wasn't close enough.

1504   Just a little bit closer, Poncho, "Whoa, whoa, aeeeee." Down, down, down splat

1505   he fell into this hole just like that. The fall should have killed him but he could feel

1506   the cold soggy sand wrapped around him like a moist blanket the sand had

1507   absorbed his fall keeping him alive. The hole as he peered up provided perfect

1508   sun light for the cave. Suddenly he was remembering his childhood, he had been

1509   here before, deja vu, how, when, he could hear the waterfall outside the cave

1510   pool, the constant splashing. He slowly eased up to his feet; he could see a bunch

1511   of sparkly things in the sand. "What are these?" He scratched at them; picked

1512   one up, spit it out. Not edible, there were thousands, he walk around the cave.

1513   He saw a white thing half buried in the sand. "What is that?" He scratched at it.

1514   More, more then he smelled, "it's my mom's skull." He leaped backward and ran

1515   to the other side of the cave. He was frightened to the core, as Poncho's memory

1516   slowly returned he and his mother had fallen into the cave. When he was a pup

1517   he remembered her leg was broken from the fall. Poncho had exhausted himself

1518   trying to figure out how to get out of this death trap. He finally flopped down on

1519   the shore of the cave pool. As he laid there he heard the whispering loud and

1520   clear. He dare not make any sudden moves. He would listen. Poncho had excellent

1521   hearing, he heard, "Do we kill him now Master?" Hundreds of tiny little glowing

1522   eyes in the roof of the cave

1523

1524   and a pool of bat poo, on the far end of the cave meant only one thing. He was in

1525   the wrong place at the wrong time. Now he had to do fast hard thinking if he was

1526   gonna live through this. How did he escape as a pup? His mother died here but he

1527   didn't. What did I do different to get outta here. He watched the sun slowly creep

1528   toward the sunset. He knew he had better be gone by sunset or those bats will

1529   make an end to him. He yelled at them. "I see you Black Fang and your whole

1530   gang." There was silence. Poncho yelled, "You hear me?" There was silence.

1531   Then the softest rustle of skin strung wings, slowly fluttered to the floor of the

1532   cave. Very large for his size, he was 75 pounds to 100 pounds of vampire bat. His

1533   large, pearl, white incisors as sharp as a needle glowing in the dark, with glowing

1534   red eyes, he folded his wing and looked at Poncho, and then he spoke: "Well, well,

1535   looks like your second visit to my quite little home." Poncho didn't reply, but

1536   listened intently as the Master of Darkness spoke. "Your mother spent many

1537   hours talking with me before she passed away. She loved you very much Poncho."

1538   Poncho said, "You are a lying gutter rat. You sucked her dry." Master of Darkness,

1539   "No, no, Poncho I did not and none of my family. Your mother

1541 begged me to save you Poncho. How do you think you survived this place?"

1542 Poncho, "Not with your help, you rotting corpse." Master, "Now, now Poncho, not

1543 so nasty right now I am the only friend you have here. My compadres want to

1544 turn you into tossed salad and red dressing," he snickered "but I won't let them."

1545 Poncho "You wanna eat me, let's tango!" Master, "No, no, Poncho you are not

1546 ready for that. You see the sun is slipping as it slips there may be change around

1547 here so listen fast. Dive in the cave pool as you did when you were a pup and

1548 swim toward the light. Do it now, or there won't be a later." Poncho was staring

1549 at Black Fang as he began to change into this black and green and orange and

1550 yellow glow in the dark. Nightmare that exploded out of its inner skin, Poncho

1551 leaped swift and fast into cave pool. "Swim towards the light." He was out of

1552 breath and strength but whoa, air, air, air, ah, ah. He crawled to the shore. "Oh

1553 my Lord what was that?" he said out loud. "That was the Dr. Jekyll and Mr. Bite

1554 you a new butt, thank goodness never again."

1555   Poncho was soaking wet and waterlogged. He gathered his strength and

1556 shook himself fast and furious to remove as much water

Chapter XXIV
Encounter
At
Red Lick

1557

1558   from his fur coat as possible. Poncho said, "Ah, ah, oh yes, feels much better,

1559   much lighter. Wow, that was a horrific experience. So that's how I got out the first

1560   time. Poor mom she suffered a horrible death, in that god for saken place at the

1561   hand of that black evil critter. One day I'll return with a solution to Black Fang and

1562   his gang of blood suckers." Then Poncho yelled, "Just wait and see. I'll be back you

1563   black hearted blood suckers."

1564   **'Lil Red's Encounter with Poncho Fox**

1565   That said he rolled up his tail and trotted into the forest. After that he was

1566   very hungry. Poncho says, "Its suppertime. Well, well, well what's on the menu,

1567   um um um oh yes tasty grouse oh yeah always nesting on the ground, easy

1568   pickings, look here there she is hiding in the tall grass, I'll slink very low in the

1569   grass, quite as a mouse, let me sneak very slowly, slowly, slowly stop! She smells

1570   me, wow I forgot to sneak down wind towards her. Swoosh, swoosh gone in a

1571   flash Jenny and Jerry Grouse flashed into the air, they spotted poncho, Jenny

1572   dropped to the ground kicking and squawking, with a pretend broke leg. Poncho

1573   yelled, "Ha, you stop faking I know that trick, I ain't fallen for that trick." He

1574   promptly strolled to her nest and gobbled all but 2 of her eggs, Poncho thinking,

1575   and "I leave those for next year."

Chapter xxv
Terriorist Attempt
at
Emerald Mound

EPISODE IV

1576   Then he moved on to the next nest. "Oh yeah, four more fresh eggs, wow

1577   that should do until I get to the fishing pond" He then trotted toward the pond.

1578   As he crossed the meadow, he stopped to rest a minute. As he rested, a familiar

1579   smell trickled down from the trees above, him oh yes. He spoke loudly, "I smell

1580   you 'Lil Red, hiding up there."

1581   There was no response again he spoke loudly, "I smell you 'Lil Red", at that

1582   "Oh, hello Poncho, I know your smell anywhere. Wow Poncho your nose is very

1583   smart and very keen." "Yep, that's why I am at the top of this food chain," he

1584   laughed. "Oh by the way," said 'Lil Red "how's the cub's?" "They are growing like

1585   weeds. Roseta has her paws full with her two sisters helping with feeding they are

1586   very busy this time of year." "Oh, wow, Poncho I almost forgot there is an

1587   emergency for you." "What?" said Poncho, "an emergency?" "Yes," said Red.

1588   "The owls were chasing Roseta all over Coon Box Fork, they had mobbed her. She

1589   is injured very badly." Poncho laughed and said, "Red you don't have to lie to me,

1590   I'm not gonna eat you." Red said, "This is no lie, Roseta is in trouble." Poncho

1591   stopped laughing and asked, "Are you serious?" "Yes," replied Red, "the last I saw,

1592   the owl Big hoots and gang chased her into the concrete flat and she got hit by a

1593   big 14 wheel monster. "

1594   **The Mobbing Attempt on Lil Red**

1595   Before Red could finish speaking, Poncho was gone. He flashed into a fox

1596   panic. Poncho hurled himself into the forest, leaping, hopping, pouncing, and

1597   dodging trees and stumps, scrambling toward his beloved Roseta. He was nearing

1598   Coon Box Fork and the air strip, where he could see those flying monsters jump in

1599   the sky. He could smell their smoke from their noise makers and see the smoke

1600   streaming from the spinning blades as the sky monsters climb in the heavy

1601   evening air.

1602   Poncho leaped across the drainage ditch, hopped, and pounced to the edge

1603   of the white stone path. Then he stopped, he could smell Roseta's blood trail

1604   scattered everywhere. "Oh no, oh no" his tail bristled, his anger flashed into fury.

1605   He snarled into furious fury as he leaped onto the stone path, "swoosh, swoosh" a

1606   4 wheeler

1607

1608   almost got him as he dashed across the blood trail of Roseta. His fury exploded in

1609   a fire ball of anger as he followed the blood trail. We must leave Poncho, and

1610   cross the valley to catch up with our beloved 'Lil Red, unaware she was being

1611   followed by Big Hoots gang. As we get closer to Red we could hear her singing,

1612   "Snake killers, ghost killers, ooh la la, holy rollers, holy rollers." Oh my gosh, at

1613   that very second, swoosh, swoosh , swoosh, slam, bang pow, Red was hit like a

1614   hammer, spinning out of control, there was an explosion of red feathers.

1615   Wounded, she managed to correct her flight screaming, "Help, help! Oh my gosh!

1616   Help, help me!" She could see Emerald Mound in the distance, flopping and

1617   flipping to avoid the owls' kamikaze style. Red was fading fast, she dove towards

1618   Emerald mound. She could see Emerald cloud standing in the doorway of his

1619   Teepee lodge, looking skyward, she was streaking towards him. Big Hoots gang

1620   was on her tail suddenly, bang! She was slammed again, an explosion of red

1621   feathers everywhere. Red felt herself falling, falling. She could see her feathers

1622   like rain falling to earth. Every thing went black. 'Lil Red awakens in a nice warm

1623   nest of hay with fresh water and a full bowl of seeds. Leaning over

1624

Chapter XXVI
Big Hoots
Declares War

1625 her nest was a friendly face she readily remembered the great Mystic of Mystics,

1626 Shaman Emerald Cloud. He spoke, "My, my, ''Lil Red, you were almost owl food,

1627 but not today and not now." She asks, "What happened?" Emerald said, "You

1628 crashed into my water pond and so did the owls, they scrambled out and flew

1629 away and I fished you out of the pond." Red was shaking and sore from her crash.

1630 For now she felt safe, snug and warm. She slipped into a deep sleep. Emerald

1631 cloud picked her little nest up and stepped out side behind his lodge, gently eased

1632 Red into the bird Teepee and closed the flap to cover the entrance. He then

1633 returned to his lodge and resumed his work. The evening slipped into darkness

1634 and the moon rose into the night sky and flung her light upon the lush green

1635 surface of Emerald mound.

1636 BIG HOOTS DEATH WARRANT AT EMERALD MOUND

1637   "Schreee, schreee, aheeee." 'Lil Red was startled to wide eyed panic. It

1638 sounded like she was surrounded thousands of chicken hungry owls. Red looked

1639 around, she was alone in the bird Teepee. Her ears led her to peek out the Teepee

1640 and she eased to the flap   and peeked out. To her surprise the owls were

1641 gathered in a giant white oak, next to the mound.

1642

Chapter XXVII
Emerald Cloud
Exposes
Jim Crow and
His Tactics

1643   Lil Red could see hundreds of them, squawking and hooting peeked out.

1644   Red lay at the doorway and listened. She heard the sound of large wings flapping

1645   as they passed over her Tee Pee. She was sure it was Big Hoot. All the squawking

1646   went silent, Big Hoot then called his gang to order, "The hunt is on. The big boss

1647   Black fang has ordered us to find those nosey critters that live on Tomahawk farm

1648   and wipe them out. Poncho fox and this varmint, Howie crow, all his comrades,

1649   except this pink, nosey critter called Chicha and her companion 'Lil Red. He wants

1650   these two brought to him alive, for deep questioning. The Boss has ordered

1651   Widow to get rid of that ugly blue mule, walk on water if needed. Ya'll got that?"

1652   then he "yelled" I find that doggone Poncho foxx and wipe him out today. now

1653   all of have your orders,," Poncho's corpse today"

1654   **Lil Red Visits Emerald Cloud at Emerald Mound**

1655   As the beautiful reddish and blues of the sky lay low on the horizon, Lil

1656   Red peeked out of her teepee with sleepy eyes. She peered into the early

1657   morning horizon, misty and blue slowly the red orb of the sun, peeked above the

1658   horizon, as 'Lil Red stretched and began to ready herself for the day.

1659   As she looked around, the village of Emerald Mound began to stir and each

1660   individual began the works of the day. Emerald Cloud stepped out of the teepee

1661   to embrace the morning sun, with prayer and worship to the Great Spirit. 'Lil Red

1662   observed him giving thanks to The Great Spirit as he kneeled towards the sun.

1663   When he finished, he arose. 'Lil Red flew from her teepee to his shoulder.

1664   Emerald Cloud said, "Well, well, well little one, I see you're feeling well

1665   enough to test your wings. That is a sign of strength returning to your wings."

1666   Little Red cooed in a small voice, "Yes great one, I am feeling better." Emerald

1667   Cloud said, "You flew all this way for a reason. What is it that you wish to know?"

1668   Red said, "We, that is my friends of Tomahawk Farms, are troubled by the

1669   protectors of the Windsor Secrets. They are always hiding in plain sight listening

1670   at every conversation around the farm and the five surrounding farms." Lil Red

1671   said, "Chicha, my friend, and I have noticed these protectors all working for the

1672   Dark Lord that calls himself Black Fang. We have never seen him but have heard

1673   through his many workers of darkness. That anyone asking questions, or

1674   discussing, or even thinking about the secrets of Windsor can become owl food,

1675   snake snack, road kill, buzzard lunch, or generally disappear without a trace. We

1676   are sick of looking over our shoulder so I am here to ask for help to locate Big

1677   Boulder, the Great Spirit eagle of the sky. We need to ask him to help protect us

1678   from this growing menace, of sneaky oppression masterminded by the Lord of

1679   Darkness, old Fang Devil himself."

1680   Emerald Cloud listened intently to 'Lil Red and there was a long silence

1681   before he spoke. Emerald Cloud said, "I have some news for you and your friends

1682   at Tomahawk Farms. Lil Red, you, Chicha, and all the other barnyard friends, are a

1683   special group of the best Blue Ribbon breeds. All of you belong to the Winsor

1684   stables in a land called Eng-land, to the Great White Mother called Queen Eliza-

1685   beth. She is responsible for you and your friends being at Tomahawk Farms and

1686   coming to this place called Win-sor. Win-sor was named by the Queen's great,

1687   great, great grandson Lord Winsor. My people, the Alcorn tribe, and our brothers

1688   the Choc-taw, remember the first family of Winsor almost froze to death and their

1689   barnyard family almost perished." Emerald Cloud said, "Lil Red, your great, great,

1690   great grandmother Big Sally Red, Big Tom, the blue mule and uncle West, the big

1691   Billy goat, and his wife Miss Julia's great, great, great grandparents were all saved

1692   by me and my people. And, to this day, that also includes the Royal Ginny Fowls,

1693   the Royal Peacocks, and a select group of Royal Egyptian Crows and the most

1694   dangerous pair of Egyptian Cobras. I want you to share this with Chicha and the

1695   others so that they can realize their value in this world and know where they came

1696   from in the old world."

1697   **Emerald Cloud said, "I wish to share the Alcorn Tribal legend with you Lil Red**

1698   **and I would like for you to share the legend with your friends. My people**

1699 believe at the birth of the sun and his sister the moon that their mother died, so

1700 the sun gave to the earth the body of his mother from which sprang all life. And

1701 he drew forth from her heart the stars. The stars he flung into the night skies to

1702 remind him of her eternal spirit. The stars missed her so much that they spread

1703 into infinity in search of her eternal spirit. Lil Red said "Emerald Cloud, what a

1704 beautiful story." Red asked, "Did the stars find her spirit?" Emerald Cloud

1705 answered, "Infinity is forever and forever is eternal." The search continues. Lil

1706 Red had tears dripping from her beak.

1707 Emerald Cloud said, "Lil Red you and the others must fight these protectors

1708 as one group to rid Tomahawk Farms and the surrounding farms of this

1709 oppression, created by this dark spirit, Black Fang."

1710 "Tell Chicha and the others to ban together and use Big Boulder and Poncho

1711 Fox and the eldest son of Don Crow ah, ah, his name is Howie to combat this

1712 growing Darkness Black Fang. Remember Lil Red, you can only win as one group.

1713 Expose them by speaking. "Hey, hello. You up there? Never let your enemies

1714 have a minutes rest hiding in plain sight. You said Lil Red, that's what Chicha said."

1715 "Oh great Emerald Cloud, yes Lil Red, Chicha is on the mark. No place to hide or

1716 spy for the Protectors."

1717   "Lil Red, before you leave to travel home know this, the secret of Winsor is

1718   not your responsibility. Do not be tricked into a hungry mind to seek this treasure,

1719   it will only bring you knowledge, grief, and pain, and disrupt your life. Tell Chicha

1720   to trust no one."

1721   "This is a cold painful end, colder than vanished hope. Tell Chicha that no

1722   one is to know this man made secret. All who learned the details have perished, it

1723   is for the Crows to bear only. It is the curse of Lord Winsor's greed, poisoned by

1724   the death and the blood of many slaves killed to protect Lord Winsor's wicked

1725   wealth and eternal poison. Lord Winsor died in the civil war. He never returned

1726   to release his dead slaves' spirits," said Emerald Cloud. "Tell Chicha to stay away

1727   from this trap and do not tell anyone anything about Howie's attempt to tell

1728   Chicha or you about the Bluewater or the Jim Crow factor or he will disintegrate

1729   into the cave pool. Tell Howie it's a trap. Now go, while the daylight is full and

1730   bright. Travel well 'Lil Red," said Emerald Cloud, "and let Big Balder Eagle combat

1731   this darkness called Black Fang."

1732   "Remember Lil Red, you can only win as one group. Expose them by

1733   speaking, "hello, you up there."whats going on" Never let your enemies have a

1734   minutes rest, hiding in plain sight. Tell Chicha trust no one.

1735   Lil Red said, "Great Mystic, what is the Jim Crow Factor? There was a long

1736   silence. Emerald Cloud took in a deep breath and spoke very softly, "Lil Red, what

1737   you ask is for me to share a cup of poison. Do you really want to know?" Lil Red

1738   nodded her head "Yes."

1739   Emerald Cloud spoke soft and clear, "To create inequality, to accept

1740   inequality enforced upon others, to deliver inequality with a clear conscience, on

1741   all designated individuals, male, female and children, to be willing to defend

1742   inequality with your last breath or your dearest blood of your own family. To

1743   accept and enforce inequality eyes wide shut. **Jim Crow is a thief of freedom, a**

1744   **killer of undiscriminating gender, an immortal being that can only be put to**

1745   **sleep or immobilized, or forgotten. A time traveler that lives in the mind of**

1746   **man, Jim Crow is the most dangerous criminal in the world."** At hearing this, Lil

1747   Red had tears rolling down her beak and her cheeks. She was trembling from

1748   head to claws. She was emotionally touched to her core. "Oh my gosh, Great

1749   Emerald Cloud, how could anyone live with that critter running around on the

1750   loose? And he is Howie's great, great, grand daddy?" Tears flowing in torrents, Lil

1751   Red broke down in trembling tears. Emerald Cloud picked her up and kissed her

1752   head and whispered, "despair not little one, Jim Crow has been captured and is

1753   slowly being put to sleep. Lil Red speaking, "I thought Howie's great, great grand

Chapter XXVIII
Lil Red
Dead At Breakfast

1754 daddy was dead?" Emerald Cloud spoke smiling, "Remember Lil Red that Jim

1755 Crow is immortal. He can be put to sleep, immobilized, or forgotten." There is no

1756 death in him. With that statement, Lil Red flew to her teepee and packed some

1757 seeds, said a prayer and flew back to Emerald Clouds shoulder. She nuzzled his

1758 ear with her beak and whispered, "Good day Great Mystic. I must travel. I will tell

1759 the others about Jim Crow."

1760   Emerald Cloud replied, "Safe journey, little sun moon spirit.   Lil Red flung

1761   herself into the bright blue morning sky! Drying her eyes from the tears of

1762   hearing the truth about Howie's family curse and Lord Winsor's treasure, she

1763   pushed the pain into the back of her mind, and focused on gaining altitude. "Ah,

1764   at last, getting better," as she climbed in the wind and lifted her into the clouds.

1765   She could see the whole valley. "My, my," thinking to herself, "how beautiful, a

1766   giant patchwork of farms and lands. What a sight." She marveled at its majesty.

1767   "How could such a beauty be watched over by such cold-hearted critters. I can't

1768   wait to tell Chicha about Jim Crow but I should not tell anyone."

1769   **THE MOBBING OF LIL RED**

1770 Lil Red was lost in thought, when, slam, bang, pow, she was hit. The sky exploded

1771 with red feathers. She was spinning out of control. She was injured. Her left wing

1772 would not work, it was broken. She tried to flap but it was hanging limp. She

1773   screamed, "Help, help." Bang, pow, slam. She could see as she flipped. It's Big

1774   Hoots, Lil Hoots and the gang that had attacked her from above and behind. She

1775   could see Tomahawk Farm. If she could glide, flap, flap in that direction. She

1776   began to fade out of consciousness. She was being mobbed. The owls were all

1777   over her – feathers were raining.

1778   To earth, Lil Red was in free fall suddenly splat, she hit something. There

1779   was loud owl squawking then, quiet, her eyes were closed; she was so weak that

1780   she could not move. "I know these voices." They seem so far away yet so close.

1781   She tried to sit up. "No, no don't move." Lil Red could not see her eyes were wet

1782   with something and would not focus. She wiped both her eyes with her wing.

1783   "Where am I? What are the blurry faces? Am I in heaven or am I dead." Then a

1784   familiar voice said, "Get back all of you. Move, let her get some air. Move it now."

1785   Red whispered, "Is that you Chicha?" "Yes, Lil Red it's me. I am right here. Can

1786   you see me?" "No," said Lil Red. "I am blind on that side. Come close." "I must

1787   tell you what Emerald Cloud said." "I don't think I'm gonna make it through this

1788   so listen fast." "No, Lil Red, no. Please don't say things like that." Tears pouring

1789   down Chicha's face, her heart, swelled up into her neck. "Please Lil Red, don't die.

1790   No, no, no." Lil red whispered, "Chicha have Miss Corine and BreGeorge take care

1791   my babies, for there is a dowry hid under my bed for them to provide for their

1792 care. Now listen fast Chicha," her voice fading, "go to Eagle Lake and make three

1793 loud whistles and two short and Big Boulder will appear. Tell him Emerald Cloud

1794 said that this honor at Aramis, the White Queen. Then, tell him about the

1795 protectors, Emerald Cloud also said. Do not listen to Howie about his family curse,

1796 for it is no secret that it is black magic poison. It will only bring death to

1797 Tomahawk Farms. Teach everyone you know to say these words, "forget Jim Crow,

1798 three times a day. Forget Jim Crow. Forget Jim Crow. Forget Jim Crow." Lil Red

1799 faded into the great mystery of eternal sleep. Chicha burst into tears and it spread

1800 over the entire barnyard. Lil Red was dead at breakfast, lying on top of the feed

1801 bin with everyone looking on in tears. Chicha was trembling within massive

1802 emotional trauma. The owls circling overhead and laughter erupted from them,

1803 "Yea well done, fella!" yelled Big Hoots. Another nosey critter knocked off, "Black

1804 Fang will be very pleased." "Now, which one of you is gonna fetch her body away

1805 from them down below?" "Oh no boss, you can count all of us out. If any of us

1806 goes down there, they're a goner." Big Hoots laughed loudly, "Yepper deper, so

1807 let's get outer here." They flung themselves into the blue and disappeared toward

1808 the fig orchard. Chicha said, "Forget Jim Crow. Forget Jim Crow." Then it

1809 manifested in Chicha's mind. "What if Jim Crow remembers us and if we forget

1810 him we won't recognize him in the future. I will never forget Jim Crow. He is too

1811   dangerous," said Chicha

1812   We must leave Lil Red and flash back to Poncho to see where his nose has led

1813   him." Poncho could see a heavy blood stain splashed on the stone path and red

1814   fur and black and gray feathers scattered everywhere. "It looks like

Chapter XXIX (Attack on Jim Crow Politics)

FigNapped - Poncho's Revenge

1815

1816   Rosetta killed a couple of her mobster owls," Poncho was thinking to himself. "Oh,

1817   yes" as he pounced over the other side of the stone path, he landed on the

1818   carcass of two dead owls, then three owls, then four owls, then six owls that

1819   Roseta had wiped out. Then his heart sunk to his shock, red fur scattered in a big

1820   circle, bits and bits of red fox fur. He tripped over the white peeled skull of his

1821   beloved Roseta. Poncho yelped, "Low down, stinking blood sucking owls. Ahooo!

1822   Ahooo! Rosetaaa." Tears poured from his eyes. He spotted her tail in the

1823   drainage ditch in bushy mode; she fought them to her last breath. Poncho flung

1824   himself into a fox fury, scratching mud, flipping in mid air, chasing his tail, kicking

1825   and gashing his teeth growling, howling, fanatical, ferocious fury. At that moment

1826   a friend of Poncho's family fluttered silently on a high perch to observe the fury

1827   Poncho was exacting on himself. He also noticed Roseta's tail, laying in the

1828   drainage ditch and the six dead owls, behind the guard rail near the edge of the

1829   stone path. Dr. Crane was amazed at Ponchos anguish and agility, flips, pouncing,

1830   wallowing, and gashing his teeth. "Poncho, hello." said Dr. Crane. No response.

1831   Poncho did not hear. Dr Crane yelled, "Haaaaaaaa!" Louder, "Haaaaa! Poncho! Yo

1832   ho!

1833   Poncho Fox!" Poncho stopped dead in his tracks. Looked left then right then he

1834   spun around in a circle. Dr. Crane yelled, "Up here. Yes, yes up here." Poncho

1835   looked up. "Oh my little friend, my dear 'lil friend Poncho I am so sorry for your

1836   loss, I understand your frenzy of anguish." Poncho screamed, "Go away Dr. Crane,

1837   go away I cannot take anymore pain, I have become death. I have become death

1838   to all that I encounter. I am at my black and darkest moment in this life." He

1839   nuzzled her scull, "Goodbye my love," tears and blood dripping from his self

1840   inflected wounds. "Goodbye my love." That said he walked through the giant

1841   water culvert, towards Coon Box Fork air way. His head was down in great pain as

1842   he passed through the Calvert and out the back side. He crossed Roseta's blood

1843   trail, he stopped and stared at it, and then he scratched dirt over the blood

1844   stained soil and continued on his way. Poncho climbed up the hill near the stone

1845   path that the air monster uses to get speed to jump into the sky. He climbed up,

1846   saw a giant stone hole with steel bars deep inside, he crawled into this hole. "Oh,

1847   yes" thinking to himself, this will do very nicely for those murderous owls. He

1848   went deeper into this trap, there were more bars deep down with a small door

1849   that clanged when he nudged it closed, it locked.

1850   **FIGNAPPED-PONCHO'S REVENGE.**

1851   **Poncho's heart swelled with anger,** he developed a devilish look, his

1852   demeanor changed to that of a fiendish wild beast. Dr. Crane flew close to the

1853 drain culvert and landed in a tree above Poncho. Dr. Crane said, "The owls have

1854 broken your heart into droplets of pain that is inconsolable, so I won't add to your

1855 contempt, but I offer a solution that may not and can never replace the loss of

1856 Roseta. I offer you those who took Roseta's life."

1857   Poncho was in tears. On hearing what Dr. Crane said, his ears perked up. He

1858 sat on his haunches and listened intently. Dr. Crane said, "Poncho, owls love rats."

1859 "So do I once in a while," said Poncho. "Well my friend, rats love figs." Poncho

1860 interrupted, "What has that got to do with this act of murder of my beloved

1861 Roseta." Dr. Crane, "Hold on, hold on, I'm getting to the point. Poncho the biggest

1862 fig orchard in this valley is across this very road at Coon Box Fork air way. The Rats

1863 are having their yearly fig jamboree from dusk till dawn. At midnight the Hoots

1864 gang shows up to dine on fat fig stuffed rats till dawn. At dawn they are so stuffed

1865 they can't fly two feet. All they can do is sit like ducks on a pond. That includes

1866 Big

1867

1868 Hoot." Pancho said, "I gotta go." "Good hunting Poncho." Dr. Crane flew away

1869 into the woods to continue his family visits to deliver a new born.

1870 Poncho sat on his haunches amazed at Dr. Crane's honesty on how to exact

1871 his revenge upon the owls. What a great way to plan his next move. Hairs

1872 standing on end, brisling, growling, scratching, clawing, at dirt in a frenzied circle.

1873 "I will make Big Hoot pay for my beloved Roseta's loss and get rid of all those

1874 rotten owls." Poncho snarled and gritted his teeth. "Well let me go survey this

1875 airway and fig orchard to get organized with a plan." Poncho walked over to

1876 Roseta's blood stains placed his paw on the stains, eyes flooding tears. He

1877 howled, "Roseta, Rosetaaaaaaaa, my love ahwooooo, ahwoooo, and

1878 ahwooooooooooooo. I will avenge you my love." He then nuzzled her blood trail.

1879 Poncho turned around and trotted out of the culvert up the hill as he got to

1880 the top he noticed a large boulder tittering on the edge of the hill, he thought this

1881 will close the trap. Poncho trotted along side the stone air strip he could see one

1882 of those metal beasts roaring down the stone path, gathering speed to jump in to

1883 the sky. At first he

Chapter XXX (Poncho's Tactics

Entrapment

of

Big Hoots

1884

1885 was afraid as it approached him, but it passed as though he was not noticed. He

1886 barked, woof, woof at it just the same to warn the steel beast he was not afraid.

1887 He raised his tail and curled it to show his dominance.

1888 Poncho could smell the fig orchard in the distance, he was close. There

1889 were these other delicious smells along the path more enticing the, smell of beef

1890 and chicken. "There it is, a place where all those two legged humans gather to sit

1891 and eat." Micky Ah, Micky Dee's. His sharp nose led him to this giant green steel

1892 box behind Micky Dee's, he wandered to its open door. To his surprise the crows

1893 and birds were all around eating and feasting on all sorts of goodies. He climbed

1894 up and jumped inside, the birds ignored him; even the crows were brazen, not

1895 afraid of his presence.

1896 "Wow," then he realized, "why this box is full of meats and half chewed

1897 meat things and sweet tasting goodies so much?" It was more than he could even

1898 eat. Poncho gorged himself on tasty meat and sweet thingies. Poncho thought to

1899 himself, it's a silo for humans. Every critter was gorging itself on all of these tasty

1900 things.

1901 Poncho noticed the sky was filling with clouds and getting dark along the

1902 horizon. He could smell the rain on its way and distant thunder rumbling in the

1903 western sky. His stomach was full bulging from all the goodies he had consumed.

1904 The darkness had crept into the sky above him. It is time to head towards his

1905 destination. Poncho turned and hopped out of the giant steel box of goodies and

1906 landed on the ground. The birds scattered to get out of his way. Full and content

1907 he continued his trek towards the fig orchard.

1908 **Rat-a-lious**

1909   He arrived at dusk; the sky was dark grayish blue. Poncho skirted around

1910 the bushes, under the barb wire fence and slinked toward the broken down

1911 building in the center of the orchard, slinked across the open yard into the side

1912 entrance of the barn, slipped up the stairs, to the second floor over looking the

1913 orchard and laid down at the edge of the door, to observe the rats feeding madly

1914 on the ripe figs that grew and dropped on the ground, which was covered with

1915 them. As the evening slipped into night Poncho fell asleep. A dream came upon

1916 him, he was being chased by two legged humans, they had fire sticks. They would

1917 boom, boom when they pointed them at him. He was galloping at full speed

1918 trying to escape but the hounds had him boxed in, so he flung himself on the

1919 lowest limb of Dead Men Dwarf. The limb came to life and screamed, "Get off of

1920 me," and slung him to another limb and that limb slung him into another tree.

1921 Then that limb broke and he fell into the brook, "Oh my, I'm drowning." He was

1922   scrambling to get to the surface, too weak. He was clawing at the water but fell

1923   deeper a paw grabbed him and pulled him to the surface for one brief second he

1924   saw Roseta's face she said do you wanna live for ever, then disappeared. He was

1925   gasping for air when he awoke with a startled jolt and banged his head on the side

1926   of the doorway, "Ouch, that hurt." He open his eyes, it was a dream. Poncho

1927   peered into the dark, the moon was full and the rats were everywhere. The trees

1928   were full of rats gorging on sweet figs. The ground was covered with rats, he could

1929   see by the light of the big yellow moon. Then there was the sound of big wings

1930   passing in front of the moon, hundreds of them. "OOOOh yesssss," said Poncho.

1931   "The owls are here." Poncho sat quietly as they landed in the tops of the fig trees,

1932   not a single owl pounced or attacked a rat. They were just sitting. Poncho,

1933   thinking to himself, "What, why are they not pouncing on these rats?" Poncho

1934   was surprised, they were just sitting an hour or so, then one very large shadow

1935   pass by the moon very large owl. "Ah, so they

1936

1937 were waiting for Big Hoot and so am I," thought Poncho. Big Hoot landed in the

1938 center tree in the orchard, settled on the top most branch, and sat quietly till the

1939 moon was mid sky. Then he raised both wings and hooted two loud long hoots,

1940 "Hootie Hootooo" and then all heck broke loose. The owls like a black hoard of

1941 winged mobsters, swooped into the orchard, there were loud squeals of rat

1942 screams and alarms from every corner of the orchard, rats being gobbled alive

1943 others being dropped mid air only to be snatched by another owl before he hit the

1944 ground. The moon light madness of rat-a-lious was so vast and violent, great

1945 horned owls by the hundreds were in a feeding frenzy, Poncho was frightened at

1946 the sight of so many owls, if they spot him he is a goner, no wonder Rosetta was

1947 torn to bits. There were owls every two inches or more. They were swooping

1948 diving, hopping rat to rat. The rats were scampering, hopping, jumping, flipping,

1949 and falling from the sky only to be gobbled before they hit the ground. Rats were

1950 leaping fig tree to fig tree. The owls were snatching rats mid jump; this went on

1951 for hours and hours. It was so intense Poncho lost track of time. He glanced at

1952 the sky, and the moon was disappearing into the horizon and the sky was turning

1953 red. "Ah-ha, day break is coming." The sky slowly turned peach, then bright red as

1954 the clouds and mist began to roll away from center of the horizon. The light slowly

1955 spread into the trees then it crept into the orchard. There were thousands of owls

1956   feasting on rats. Some were sprawled out on their backs, too full to move, stuffed

1957   on rat meat. Others were asleep in the trees, others still feasting. Poncho, ears

1958   back peeking thru the door cracks in the barn, so not to expose himself, looked for

1959   Big Hoot. "Where is he?" Looking peering sharply, hi and lo, no Big Hoot. Then

1960   out of the corner of his eye, he saw a big feather blob walking on the ground

1961   staggering from side to side, as though it were drunk or wounded. He was headed

1962   toward the center tree in the orchard, too heavy to fly. Poncho flung himself

1963   around, down the stairs, out the back door, slinked across the yard to the bushes,

1964   down the fence line using the bushes to skirt around to the center of the orchard

1965   he was using his foxy slyness to the max. Poncho slinked as close as possible to his

1966   target, he kept his eyes locked on Big Hoot. Slippery as a slinky fox, he slipped

1967   under the big green hedge across from the tree in the center of the orchard. Big

1968   Hoot was staggering around the base of the giant oak tree, he spread his huge

1969   wings and began to flap, as fast as he could. At that moment Poncho panicked, he

1970   almost sprang from his hiding place, to grab Big Hoot. That would be a mistake.

1971   He maybe overweight but remains very dangerous with killing claws and a very

1972   powerful beak for ripping flesh. Poncho cannot afford to make a mistake, so

1973   Poncho waited for the moment, thinking to himself timing is everything at this

1974   moment. Big Hoot could not lift his over stuffed body to become airborne. He

1975	flapped and flapped and flapped he began to flap frantic, burning all of his
1976	strength. Poncho snickered to himself, "Yes sir, yes sir, he's wore himself out." At
1977	that moment, Big Hoot collapsed on his back. Totally worn out, he was breathing
1978	hard and very weak. He lifted himself off of his back and sat up facing the tree,
1979	heaving for his next breath. "Yep," said Poncho to himself, "too many rats in your
1980	gullet." At that moment Poncho sprung from his hiding place. Leap, leap, pounce,
1981	he grabbed Big Hoot from the back of his neck. "Wow," Poncho thought "this was
1982	perfect timing." Big Hoot was so shocked he began flapping and flapping wildly.
1983	Poncho had him pinned by his most vulnerable point, on the back of his neck,
1984	almost impossible to get this position, when an owl this size is fully awake.
1985	Poncho was growling and furious, his strength was at max he snatched Big
1986	Hoot like feather in mid air, and disappeared back into the hedge and bushes that
1987	he had sprung from. Big Hoot could not scream, he was shocked and Poncho had
1988	almost choked his airway. He could not scream for help, caught from behind , he
1989	could not claw or bite. Poncho snickered to himself, "Yes, I got you now Big Hoot."
1990	Poncho was speeding on the outside of the fence of the fig orchard, fleeing
1991	towards the airway stone path, he was half way there, when Big Hoot's heavy
1992	weight began to fatigue on Poncho's neck, but he dare not release his grip on this
1993	dangerous owl. Big Hoot growled, "Put me down you brigand, put me down right

1994   now, or I'll rip you to red fur balls." Poncho growled between his teeth, "You

1995   ripped my beloved Rosetta. You snake, I am gonna turn you into a big gray feather

1996   duster," said Poncho. Big Hoot said, "Oh yes, your here to avenge her death,

1997   mighty noble of you, but foolish. Me and my gang are gonna do to you what we

1998   did to Roseta. We enjoyed every scrap of her tender sweet meat. Yes, yes, we

1999   chased the sweet tasting young fox all over Coon Box Fork. She was so confused.

2000   She ran on to that stone path right into a big red 14 wheeled monster. It finished

2001   what we started, we drug her smashed body onto the road side and ripped the

2002   tasty parts out we feasted on everything but her big red tail and when I get loose,

2003   I'm gonna rip out your juicy sweet eye balls and eat them whole while you are

2004   looking at me." Poncho was losing his grip on Big Hoots neck, he was dragging Big

2005   Hoot. Poncho stopped to adjust his hold on Big Hoot, thinking to himself, "I must

2006   be careful, one second and rebite." Big Hoot jumped loose from Poncho's tight

2007   grip long enough to scream, two loud screams, "Help help, hooti, hoooo, hooti,

2008   hooo." Poncho was quick, he grabbed Big Hoot by the skin of his neck unblocking

2009   Big Hoot airway, Big Hoot began screaming loud long hoots and squawk squawk

2010   squawks squawks. "Hoot who hooti-hoo squawk." Within seconds Poncho could

2011   hear the return squawk answering Big Hoots squawks for help Poncho's hearing is

2012   excellent. He could hear the return squawks getting closer. Big Hoot was

2013   squawking frantic screams. Poncho went to full speed fox trotting mixed with

2014   leaping pronks. Big Hoot growled, "Yes, yes, Poncho we're gonna, rip you a new

2015   butt, you 'lil red fox devil." Poncho slammed Big Hoot against the light pole,

2016   wham, wham, "Shut up you

Chapter XXXI (The Anesting of Jim Crow)

The-Gurgling-Sound

of

Owls

2017

2018   gray ball of puke." Wham, wham, against each light pole as Poncho passed.

2019   Poncho said, "I'm gonna beat the gray feathers off your dead corpse and make a

2020   feather duster for my den, you dust ball." Poncho could see the stone culvert, only

2021   a few more feet. Poncho could hear the beat of hundred of big wings on his tail,

2022   he glanced over his shoulder and, oh my, thousands of owls were right on him as

2023   he leaped into the culvert and dashed to the far end. The owls squawking and

2024   screaming piled into the culvert. Crawling, clawing, and scrambling deep into the

2025   culvert to rescue Big Hoot. Poncho, dragged Big Hoot into the iron bars and

2026   stuffed Big Hoot between the bars and slammed the iron gate closed on Big Hoot.

2027   It locked, Big Hoot screamed, "You red fur ball, I will hunt you down and pick your

2028   eyes out with my claws one at a time, and strangle you with your eye ball cord!"

2029   Poncho yelled, "Never, over my dead rotting corpse! This is the end of you, and

2030   your gang." Poncho's voice was echoing in the culvert, the owls were every where

2031   in the tunnels. Poncho slipped between the bars out the rear of the culvert, and

2032   peeked up to see if any owls were standing guard. Thinking to himself, "I am a

2033   lucky lil fox." They were all piled into the culvert

2034

2035 searching for Big Hoot squawking loud at the bottom of the culvert. Poncho

2036 snickered to himself, "That's it; all of you crowd into the hole." Poncho peeked

2037 over the top of the culvert then looked up at all the surrounding trees, not a single

2038 owl sentinel, or watch owl. Poncho slipped over the top of the culvert, all of the

2039 owls screaming and squawking were in the culvert, trying to save Big Hoot.

2040 Poncho eased close to one of the many, giant boulders tittering on the edge of the

2041 hills above the culvert entrance. With all the strength he could muster, Poncho

2042 pushed on this boulder and it rolled slightly, then he pushed more it rolled over

2043 the edge of the hill and rolled down, down, and down, bang, clunk, clunk, into the

2044 culvert hole blocking the entrance. Poncho flung himself down the hill and into

2045 the culvert ditch and pushed the boulder in farther to block the entrance. Poncho

2046 could feel the rain drops drip dropping on his head, dripping faster, then thunder,

2047 closer more thunder, then down pour. Poncho yelled around the bolder, "Haaa,

2048 y'all looking for me? You low life gray feather dusters!" The owls were squawking

2049 at the boulder, screaming angry slurs at Poncho. The rain began to pour into

2050 torrents, the ditch began to fill with water, all draining from the stone path air

2051 strip. "Oh yes," yelled Poncho. "This is for Rosetta. Awoooo, awoo, Rosettaaa.

2052 You gray blood suckers you will never kill another fox cause your all gonna drown.

2053   Drown you blood sucker, drown!" yelled Poncho. The ditch filled to a flood then

2054   over flowing flood level Poncho began an indian rain dance. There was loud

2055   squawking, then screams for help then gurgling, flapping, flapping frantic flapping

2056   and screaming squawks. Then silence, Poncho, dancing in the rain a wild Irish jig,

2057   hopping, fox trotting in a circle. This is for you Rosetta, pronking high in the air

2058   leaping pronks in the rain. He began to sing, "I am dancing in the rain, I am

2059   dripping wet from owl crocket, I am dripping wet from owl crocket, ding dong the

2060   wicked owls are dead." Poncho danced for hours. Trotting toward home and

2061   dancing all the way whistling "I'm dancing in the rain, I'm dancing in the

2062   rainnnnnnnn," as Pancho's voice faded into the forest.

2063   The End

2064

2065

Chapter XXXII (Our Story Continues)
The Legend
of
Orecal
at
Winsor Ruins

From the Author,

Our sincere thanks to the next pages of contributors to the completion
of this works of art listed and unlisted on the following pages.
To order a list of book, email Dwarfcorp@aol.com

Thank you,
Dwarf Communication Corp.

2066   "OUR STORY CONTINUES IN THE LEGEND OF ORECOL AI DEADMEN DWARF AI

2067   WINSOR RUINS. ORDER YOUR COPY AT   WWW.TRAFFORD.COM   OR

2068   ----E-mail us at   Dwarfcorp@aol.com   query book titles. To order Internet

2069   query www.Traffordbooks.com 1-888-232-4444 or1-866-941-0370

2070   Author Parker Chamberlain

2071   Illustrator Parker Chamberlain

2072   **Executive Editor Jamie L. Lail**
                       Asst. Holly Steck

2073

2074

2075

2076

2077   EXPLORE OUR WEB SITE COMING SOON WWW DEAD MEN DWARF .COM

2078   Episode 1 order WWW TRAFFORD. COM

2079   Episode2

2080   Episode 3

2081   Explore OTHER BOOKS AND E-BOOK BY PARKER CHAMBERLAIN

2082   Bibliography: FOR DEAD MEN DWARF AT WINDSOR RUINS

2083   AS THE AUTHOR I WISH TO EXPRESS MY THANKS TO THE CONTRIBUTORS LISTES
2084   BELOW

2085   FOR THERE PHOTOGRAPHS PERIDIOCALS AND OTHER CONTRIBUTIONS THAT
2086   PROVIDED   REFERENCE INFORMATION FOR THE COMPLETION OF THESE
2087   BOOKS FIRST EDITON, SECOND EDITION AND THIRD EDITIONS, THANK YOU FROM

2088	PARKER CHAMBERLAIN FOR HELPING ME PROVIDE ELEMENTS TO COMPLETE
2089	THESE WORKS OF ART.
2090	
2091	
2092	1. NATIONAL PARKS SERVICE, PHOTOGRAPHS OF NATCHEZ TRACE
2093	PARKWAY AND PHOTO GALLERY OF HISTORICAL FARMS ALONG THE
2094	PARKWAY
2095	
2096	2. US DEPARTMENT OF INTERIORS FOR PHOTO GALLERY, FARM HOMES
2097	AND BARNS OF AMERICA
2098	
2099	
2100	3. MISSISSIPPI BATTLE FIELD TOUR PHOTO GALLERY OF WINDSOR RUINS
2101	AND ASSOCIATED PHOTOGRAPHS OF EMERALD MOUND ON THE
2102	NATCHEZ TRACE PARKWAY
2103	
2104	4. US DEPARTMENT OF INTERIORS FOR PHOTO GALLERY PHOTOGRAPHS
2105	OF MOUNT LOCUST AND PHOTOS OF CHURCH STREET IN PORT GIBSON
2106	MISSISSIPPI
2107	
2108	
2109	5. CATALINA GARCIA FOR PHOTOGRAPHS OF DWARF TREES AT WINDSOR
2110	RUINS
2111	
2112	6. CATALINA GARCIA FOR PHOTOGRAPHS OF WINDSOR RUINS SIXTEEN
2113	COLUMNS
2114	
2115	
2116	7. MISSISSIPPI BATTLE TOURS PHOTO GALLERY FOR CHURCH STREET PORT
2117	GIBSON MISSISSIPPI AND ALL BATTLE FIELD TOUR MARKER SIGNS
2118	UTILIZED FOR HISTORICAL VALUE
2119	

2120   8. TRAVEL IMAGES.COM FOR PHOTOS OF PHAR MOUNDS FALL HOLLOW
2121   FOR FARM PHOTOGRAPHS
2122
2123

2124   9. SHUTTER STOCK.COM FOR FARM PHOTOGRAPHS
2125

2126   10. THE HONORABLE DAVID L GREEN, STATE REPRESANTIVE MISSISSIPPI
2127   LEGISLATURE FOR FAMILY CONTRIBUTIONS FOR THE COMPLETION OF
2128   THIS WORK
2129
2130

2131   11. MISSISSIPPI LEGISLATURE VIA INTERNET INFORMATION THAT PROVIDED
2132   HISTORICAL BACKGROUND FOR THIS WORK
2133

2134   12. ALL CORN STATE UNIVERSITY FOR PHOTOGRAPHIC HISTORY OF ITS
2135   DEVELOPMENT
2136
2137

2138   13. CITY OF FAYETTE HISTORICAL CONTRIBUTION AND BIRTH PLACE OF THE
2139   AUTHOR PARKER CHAMBERLAIN FOR PHOTOGRAPHIC CONTRIBUTIONS
2140

2141   14. CITY OF VICKSBURG FOR PHOTOGRAPHIC CONTRIBUTIONS AS THE
2142   HOME OF AUTHOR PARKER CHAMBERLAIN
2143
2144

2145   15. THE STATE OF MISSISSIPPI FOR PHOTOGRAPHIC OPPORTUNITY OF
2146   VICKSBURG BATTLE FIELD PHOTOGRPAHS ACQUIRED BY AUTHOR
2147   PARKER CHAMBERLAIN
2148

2149   16. TOWN OF LORMAN MISSISSIPPI FOR PHOTOGRAPHIC CONTRIBUTIONS
2150   OF LANDSCAPE PHOTOGRAPHS OF ALL CORN STATE UNIVERSITY
2151
2152

2153   17. TOWN OF PORT RODNEY MISSISSIPPI FOR HISTORICAL BACKGROUND OF
2154   WINDSOR PLANTATION
2155

2156   18. US DEPARTMENT OF INTERIORS PHOTOS AND BACKGROUND OF PORT
2157   RODNEY AND WINDSOR RUINS
2158
2159

2160   19. TOWN OF PORT GIBSON FOR PHOTOS OF CHURCH STREET AND THE
2161   FAMOUS PRESBETERIAN CHURCH WITH THE GOLDEN HAND AND ALL
2162   THE OTHER HISTORICAL CITY MARKERS THAT CONTRIBUTED TO THIS
2163   WORK OF ART
2164

2165

2166   20. PHOTO GALLERY OF PARKER CHAMBERLAIN THAT CONTRIBUTED TO THE
2167   COMPLETION OF THIS WORK.
2168
2169

2170   FROM PARKER CHAMBERLAIN

2171   THE AUTHOR OF DEAD MENS DWARF AT WINDSOR RUINS,

2172   THANK YOU FOR YOUR CONTRIBUTIONS TO THE COMPLETION OF THIS
2173   WORK.

2174

Self Development

Institute for

Rosa   Parks

Civial Rights   Activist

1950   2005

Illustrated: 6/1/10
by Parker Chamberlain

Getting Into The Flow:

Author: Parker Chamberlain

We Hope You Enjoyed Dead Men's Dwarf at Winsor Ruins!

"On The Road Home..."

Coffey/Coffie Family Reunion
July 2010 -Fayette /Natchez, Mississippi

"On The Road Home..."

Coffey/Coffie Family Reunion
July 2010 -Fayette /Natchez, Mississippi

The story of West James and Julia coffee James was lived out in this intrepid plantati on house as you look at this picture it is a reminder that our lives and life works are finite, as you look at this picture you don't see the years of barbe Q's, parti es. Planti ng green gardens, picking tomatoes beans corn, okra, hide-n-go seek games we played happy and sad times. Those moments are compressed into our minds, the grand children of this couple. My grand children will only see this broken down rusting weathered hulk of a house in this book because ti me has erased this home but the families that were born in this home are flourishing and scattered around America, Milton L. James and Shelly James. and Hester James Chamberlain are the down line slave descendants of the this family, that has produced Teachers, Doctors Lawyers, Dentist, politicians, and many others, because of REAL TREASURE, EDUCATION, OUR PARENTS, STEPPED UP, AND REMINDED THEIR CHILDREN, NEVER FORGET JIM CROW IS IMMORTAL, AND PREYS ON IGNORANCE.

Folklore Art

THE LEGEND OF
DEAD MEN DWARF
AT WINSOR RUINS

and the Legend of Blue Water Treasure

PARKER CHAMBERLAIN

Educational tool to increase knowledge

TEA

Texas Education Agency
Student Assessment Directory
For Home Study Links Call (512)-463-9536

NOTE: The English and Spanish versions of STAAR assess the same reporting categories and TEKS standards.

STAAR TEKS LINKS available at this number

Students - Parents - Teachers

Utilize this links to increase children's learning capability. This link will provide additional testing tools for better test grades.

(512)-463-9536

DWARF CORP.

CREATIVE AUTHORS

FRIENDS of the Library

To the Executive librarian, this is a gift to the library from Parker Chamberlain, author of "Dead Men Dwarf at Winsor Ruins," Episodes I, II, III, IV, a series of short stories written about my childhood, growing up in Mississippi during the late fifties and transitional 60s. I wish you to display this gift and add it to your card catalog. So many others who have a great story may enjoy the rich history of my life, mix with a little Mark Twain's humor and a bit of Edgar Allan Poe's darkness.

Your library will receive Future Productions. The next issues of "The Last Chickasaw" is in Production Episode I, II, III, IV, V, VI.

Please use the web page attached to get more stories by Author Parker Chamberlain at TraffordPublishing.com bookstore
ISBN – 10:1466 945 923/Hard copies/Soft copies/E-book

Also: Ava – Audio Book   At DwarfCorp@aol.com
On Request: - MP3   Email request, special order
                        CDs   to Audio Book.
                                           Include your email, return
                                           address and phone.

Happy Reading

Thank You,
Parker Chamberlain, Author CEO
Dwarf Corp. Creative Authors

Parker Chamberlain was born during the late 50's in Fayette, Mississippi, during a time when Jim Crow was the most dangerous criminal in America, Parker Chamberlain is a, native of Vicksburg, Mississippi. He like most American witnessed the Vietnam war, the political destruction and assassination of John F Kennedy and Bobby Kennedy and the assassination of Dr. Martin Luther King, and hundreds of individual micro cosms of change, all across America, birth pains of change, political war, water gate. Iran kuntra scandal, the moon landing. Ten presidents elected and the most surprising event in American history, the 44th president elected to office Barack Obama, the first black American president, proof positive that education and political activeness and a life death struggle with Jim Crow politics, changed the civil rights and political face of a nation. At her best, stars and stripes waiving in the winds and her worst, fire hoses blasting people in the streets in Selma, Alabama in the 60s, witnessing these events, will make Parker Chamberlain a great author through the 21st century.

The social and political change that began with the emancipation proclamation from the 1800's thru the 1900's, brought political change and self realization to the Negro's, that education was not just a dream, but a doorway that accessed the stair well to power in America; a clear message Unlocked by President Kennedy in the 1963 and 1964 Voting Rights Act, to young Black Americans that a turning point has been achieved. It began with 40 acres and a mule and has climaxed at the 44th president, a Black American; Barrack-O-bama, proof positive that America has reached her turning point. Envoked by Dr. Martin Luther King I Have a dream, America has more work ahead. Parker Chamberlain has spun a beautiful story of the Achievement of the American Experience not a Fiction, but a true story of his families American experience. Touch by the divine the Real Hunt For Treasure is Education, Political Activeness in The Communities of Our America.

Dead Men Dwarf at Windsor Ruins Teachers Key

Internet Group Activities: Research, other burial mound. Discuss the purpose designs throughout the world includes the Great Pyramid of Egypt.

Collect: Five-page essay about these burial system, grade on contents, details, contents, assembly and comprehension.

The research continues: Trafford.com for more of the author Parker Chamberlain

Disclaimer: Parker Chamberlain

As with all education products, the author created this product as a training system for simple assessment of reading, writing entertainment, its educational values is ascertained by the user of this product.

Illustration: Parker Chamberlain
Copyright: Parker Chamberlain
Copyright date: January 2012
All rights reserved: Parker Chamberlain and Catalina Cantu Garcia

Printed in the United States
by Baker & Taylor Publisher Services